Praise for Dana Landers'

"I enjoyed the way that Dana Landers entertwined all the characters in this book. Thanks much for an enjoyable collection of dog stories."

"Dana is good at creating the unhurried feelings you experience in small-town America. That sweet peace that comes from experiencing life's small everyday pleasures. Watching a child laugh as she plays with a dog; the joy that comes from memories of past joyful dog days. Reading these stories is like experiencing a beautiful peaceful dream."

"Touching, at times funny, other moments heart-breaking...as another reviewer has mentioned, make sure to have some tissues handy for this one."

"Bear is the finest dog book I have ever read. I could feel every emotion of love and connection to our best friends. This story stays with me and I want to read more of Dana Landers books. This author knows how dogs come into our lives, teach us many lessons of love, patience, trust and then leave when their job is done. I highly recommend this book to anyone who loves animals and knows how they can change their lives for the better."

CONNECTED SOULS

BY

Dana Landers

©2012

Note from the author

Although this short story is a work of fiction, it is based on a true story from my own life. I believe that quite often dogs that we have loved and that have loved us return to us in different forms. With this belief, I carry the memory of each and every one of the dogs that I have loved in my heart forever.

On Feb. 10, a dog named Cujo was surrendered to the Westfield animal shelter. Also on Feb 10. in a Westfield home, a dog named Codi said his final goodbye to the family he had loved for over 10 years. This is the story of their connected souls.

Chapter 1: Codi

It had been a long day of whining, grumpy kids. Providing home daycare was a job that Karen usually loved, but today had been one of those days that made her wonder if she wasn't getting too old for it all. She was over 50, after all! And she had been doing this job for nearly thirty years! She also knew that a lot of how she was feeling had to do with it being winter and the fact that everybody was suffering from a bit of cabin fever. Just the same, whatever the reason, it was starting to wear her down. But as it did every day, the hands of the clock finally made their way to 6 and the last tired child was sent off in the loving arms of equally weary parents. "Just a bit of clean up to do," Karen thought to herself, and she could begin her evening.

The first thing on the agenda every night was a walk with Codi, her Spaniel, Border collie cross. He was a shaggy little thing, all brown, black and white fur, with a long tail, floppy ears and short stocky legs. The kids had picked him from the litter for just that reason. They laughed at how his little legs couldn't even get him up the first steps of the front porch. They also loved his chubby little puppy belly which he had somehow never managed to outgrow.

But short legs or not, he was always ready for a walk, and he did his best to make sure it was never forgotten. For that reason alone, Karen's daily routine seldom changed. Every night after she shut off the lights, closed the door and headed upstairs from the daycare, he would be in the exact same spot. She knew he would be there, waiting at the top of the stairs, stretched out with front paws dangling down over the top step, nosed pressed against the gate, tail sweeping a clean spot across the hardwood floor, and eyes bright with anticipation.

"Are we going now?" he seemed to say. "I've been waiting for you. Let's go."

And regardless of how tired she was, or what kind of a day it had been, she couldn't resist those eyes. She would bundle up for the cold and snow while Codi watched and waited. He never seemed to quite understand what took her so long or why she had to put on so many things in order to go out when he was always at the ready to just run out the door.

"If I had your fur coat," she would say, "I could just walk out the door too!"

But he would wait patiently knowing that eventually she would be ready. It was with these thoughts in mind that Karen finally flicked off the last light switch and closed the downstairs door. As she came around the landing to head upstairs, she was surprised to see that Codi wasn't there. "Where are you old fellow?" she called. "This winter weather got you down too? Am I going to get a reprieve from walking today?"

When even her cheerful comments didn't bring him to the top of the stairs, Karen began to worry. At 10, Codi was getting on and he had been moving a bit slower these past few months. The deep, thawing snow posed a particularly difficult challenge for his short little legs this time of year. At times she would almost have to lift his back end out of the snow if he sank down too far. But he was a determined fellow, and he loved his walks! So it was quite natural for Karen to be concerned when he wasn't waiting there ready to go. Karen continued to the top of the stairs and unlatched the child gate at the top.

"Codi!" she called. "Ready for a walk?" Now she could see him. He was lying in the center of the carpet looking at her and wagging his tail but making no move to get up. "What's wrong Codi? Come here boy. It's walk time." Karen tapped her leg in a typical come here motion. The response she received was not at all what she had hoped for. She watched with dismay as Codi tried to stand up and come to her. Struggle as he might, he couldn't get up on all four legs. He could drag his back end but he couldn't stand. His eyes were still the same, full of hope and anticipation but there was something else there too, a sadness maybe, or perhaps an apology. Like he was trying to tell her that he wasn't going to be able to make it this time; that things weren't going to be the same anymore. Karen fell to her knees beside him, stroking his head and feeling the tears start to come.

"Oh buddy, what's happened? You were fine this morning. You were fine when I let you out this afternoon." Karen just sat there on the floor for the longest time, crying and petting her beloved companion. When Will, her husband came in from work, that is how he found them. Trying not to cry, Karen explained the situation and Will called their vet at the Westfield Animal Hospital. Dr. Jameson agreed to see them, and made the arrangements for Codi to come in for an emergency examination. Karen's heart sank as she watched Will carry that furry ball of love out to the car. She knew it was bad. She felt it down to the depths of her soul. And she knew that Codi felt it too. In just the blink of an eye, things were suddenly so different. There was no denying the fact that life was going to change tonight forever.

Will returned in less than an hour. He carried Codi in and placed him on his bed in the corner of the living room. The news was every bit as bad as Karen had known it would be. Dr. Jameson had told Will that a nerve was severed in Codi's spine and that his back legs could no longer function. It was possible, he said, that the strain of walking through the deep snow may have accelerated a condition that had already began to progress. Or it may have happened suddenly one time when he slipped trying to get up. There was no way to ever know for sure. The fact of the matter was, he couldn't stand, couldn't walk, and basically couldn't get around except by dragging his back end. The good news was that he was not in any pain. Surgery was an option, albeit a very expensive one, and would require the amputation of both back legs. Codi would then need to be fitted for a custom cart that would hold up his back end and roll forward as he moved his front legs. It seemed like a very complicated and unnatural way to move.

The vet was blunt and told Karen and Will to consider very carefully what Codi's quality of life would be like. And in addition to all of that, there was Codi's age to consider. Also, as Dr. Jameson pointed out, Codi had never quite been back to normal from the bladder stone surgery he had had the year before. His system was not as good as it might need to be to face surgery. The vet was being honest when he told them of the risks of the surgery and the chance that Codi's system would not be able to withstand the stress. The other option, of course, was putting Codi down. Neither Karen nor Will wanted to make that final call. They had been down this road before but never had they ended up there so suddenly and without any mental preparation. This time there was no lengthy illness or failing health to give them some time to adjust to what was coming. This time they had to make the call even when everything else about their beloved friend seemed perfectly fine. Everything except the fact that he could no longer walk!

But in the end, to do their best by their faithful, loyal friend, that was the decision they made.

They made the appointment for the following morning and took Codi home for one last goodbye from the rest of the family. The ride home was quiet and their hearts were heavy. This would be their last night together. Once they were in and had Codi settled on a blanket in the living room, Karen started making calls to her daycare parents. Daycare would be cancelled for the next day. Fortunately it was a Friday, so the weekend would be free as well. With business matters taken care of, they sat quietly together reminiscing about Codi's puppy days, his antics growing up, and all the wonderful ways in which he had enriched their lives. One by one the children went off to bed and Karen and Will sat with Codi a while longer. It was difficult getting him outside to relieve himself, but they did their best. Cody knew things weren't right. He sensed the sadness that now filled the house that was usually so happy and he knew that he was the reason. He tried with his eyes to let them know that everything would be ok. That they were making the right decision and one that he was grateful for. He so wished he could talk to them and tell them that he was looking forward to crossing over the Rainbow Bridge. He was full of anticipation of things to come. But he wanted to tell them too, that he was sorry to be leaving them. He also wanted to somehow let them know, that even though he would no longer be with them as the dog they knew, he would be with them still through the spirit of a dog that they were soon to know.

But sadly, dogs have no voice for human language. So he lay quietly, accepting their hugs and scratches, returning their love as best he could with a gentle lick of the hand or a paw resting on their leg. It was a long, strange night for Codi and his family, one of the longest Karen could remember. But when morning came, they went together to say their final goodbyes.

Chapter 2: Cujo

It was just before 9 when Becky drove into the parking lot of the Westfield animal shelter. A light winter rain was falling and coated her windshield between swooshes of the wipers. As she got closer, her stomach tightened at the sight of the large crate sitting beside the door. "Looks like we have another one," she said to herself. Though she had worked at the shelter for over eight years, she never got used to the way people could just abandon an animal that they had owned and cared for.

She didn't understand why people couldn't at least bring the dogs into the shelter instead of just dropping them off when the shelter was closed. There was never enough information about the surrendered animal when they did it this way. There would be so little information to pass along to perspective new owners. Nothing about his personality that would help match him up with the right family. Nothing, either good or bad that they could use to help make him more adoptable, to increase his chances of finding that perfect, happy forever home that he so deserved. Nothing. Just a few words scratched on a piece of paper. Sometimes they didn't even get that. It was always so sad when it happened this way.

She hoped he had only been there a while and not all night. She opened the car door and walked slowly towards the large wire cage "Hello there big guy," Becky said in a calm voice, as she approached the cage. "Aren't you a handsome fellow?" He was a fairly large dog and obviously of mixed breed. He sported black, brown and white markings very similar to a Bernese mountain dog, but with a more slender build. His nose looked almost like that of a German shepherd, but his ears were all floppy like a retriever. He was tall with a long black tail and fuzzy tan britches. The most unusual thing about him was the one ear that sat sideways atop his head as though it had forgotten which way to go. It gave the dog a very bewildered look that made you want to hug him all the more. "Well now," said Becky, "Let's just see what this note says about you."

Scrawled on a small piece of paper tied to the wire crate were these few words: "This dogs' name is Cujo. He is almost a year old and just got too big for our house and our kids. I hope you can find him a good home. Thanks."

That's it. That's all she wrote. Becky sighed and looked into the sad brown eyes and wondered what his story really was, and why on earth anyone would name a family pet Cujo! He certainly looked anything but mean or aggressive.

"Oh well," she thought. "Doesn't really matter. From here on in it's you and me and the rest of the staff. And hopefully, soon a new home with new owners."

There was a long red leash attached to the black collar around the dog's neck. Becky talked to him for a bit just to judge his reaction to her presence. When it appeared he was going to be quite docile, she slowly opened the door of the crate, talking in a reassuring tone the whole time. Cujo made no move to exit the crate, even when Becky tugged gently on the leash and urged him to come. It was obvious he had trust issues and was afraid of new situations. Becky knew that patience would be the key. She just kept talking and gradually came close enough to pat his head. When he immediately drew back, Becky did too.

"Ok fella," she said, "Nobody here is going to hurt you. Let's just get you out of this crate and inside the shelter." She wanted to get him in and settled before all the staff started to arrive. She had a sense that the chatter and bustle of everyone coming in might really scare this poor guy. With a bit more coaxing she was able to get him to walk with her. They stopped briefly by the walk and Cujo relieved himself on the bushes. "There you go," said Becky. "See, everything is ok. You are going to be fine.

We're going to take really good care of you."

Cujo was glad to get out of the crate and stretch. He had been scared and cold sitting there all by himself, wondering if anyone was going to come. Even when his people had shut him in the small room every day, it had not been as lonely as being outside in the cold dark of early morning. He wondered where his people had gone, and why they had left him here. Would they return to take him home soon? Didn't they want him anymore? He had tried to be a good dog. He had stayed quiet in the small space every day, never barking or scratching at the door. He even tried not to urinate if he could help it, but sometimes the days were just too long and he had to go. When that happened, he always went to the farthest corner of the small place, and only as often as was absolutely necessary. He never wanted to make his people unhappy.

Lately, though, he had heard the woman person complaining that he was getting too big. He had always felt in his heart that she was unhappy with him, and kind of angry with the man for bringing him home. "He is way too big to play with the kids now," she would say. "And way too big for this tiny house." This made him very sad. He loved to play with his kids and always tried to be extra careful. But maybe he hadn't been careful enough. Maybe the woman person had finally had enough and now they had left him here.

He didn't know where or what this place was, but this kind girl who was taking him out of the crate seemed very nice and gentle. Her soft voice was comforting and he wasn't afraid of her at all. The room where she took him was warm, and bright. It was clean and yet still smelled of lots of other dogs and animals. He was somewhat confused by the feelings that were coming at him from the other dogs. There seemed to be both a sense of hope and of sadness.

Later during his time here, he would learn the reason for those two emotions. There was a sense of gladness for those friends that had moved on to new homes and families, and a sorrowful kind of hope for those who were granted passage to a different place. Although their lives here on this earth had been cut short, they would now able to move forward to a new place; a place where they could begin their journey across the rainbow bridge to the land where all dogs live free from worry, illness and pain. Cujo knew that it was his time now to sit and wait. In the end, it would be one or the other of those same fates that would be his. For now, though, he was happy to be safe, warm and cared for in what he chose to call his "in between" place. The place he heard others refer to as "the shelter."

Chapter 3: Grieving

It was a warm day for mid-February and raining lightly when Karen and Will pulled into the animal hospital parking lot. The smell of spring was in the air, a smell that usually brought a sense of new beginnings and anticipation of summer. But not today. Today it seemed unfair that the weather should be so nice. A bitter cold blustery day would better suit their mood for sure. When they arrived at the hospital, Karen stood in the rain and talked to Codi through the opened back hatch of their SUV. He was curled up on his favorite blanket sniffing in great gulps of the spring like air.

His eyes never left Karen's as they tried so hard to communicate their last thoughts to each other. Codi wanted her to know that he was ok. That this was how things were meant to be, and that soon, they would find themselves comforted by the love of a new canine companion.

Karen wanted Codi to know how much she loved him, would always love him; and that he had done a wonderful job as a friend, guardian and companion. She stroked his head gently and waited for Will to return. He had gone ahead to find out where the vet wanted them to take Codi with as little exposure as possible to the other waiting patients and their owners.

Will returned shortly and said it was time. He gently lifted Codi from the blanket and carried him inside to a quiet room. Karen grabbed Codi's blanket and followed, eyes down, not wanting to look at the other dogs that were there. Other dogs that would be going home with their owners today to continue their normal lives. She followed Will into the office. Codi was placed on his blanket on the table. The vet spoke to them briefly, explaining with genuine compassion, how things would happen, and what to expect. He explained how Codi would receive two injections. One now, to relax and calm him, and a final one which would stop his heart. The vet administered the first needle and then left them alone with Codi for a few moments to say their final goodbyes. When he returned, second needle in hand, he asked if they were ready. Will nodded and the doctor looked to Karen. Tears began to fall as Karen nodded her ok. Then she knelt at Codi's head and looked straight into his eyes as the final needle was delivered. Karen watched as Codi's eyes began to droop, just as they always had when he dropped off to sleep.

He opened them one last time after the final needle was given. Karen could feel his love and knew that he felt hers. She stroked his head and sobbed as his eyes closed once again for the last time. She continued to pet him while the vet used a stethoscope to check his heart. She laid her head against his, her tears wetting the soft brown fur, as the vet's words stabbed into her heart. "Codi's gone," he said quietly.

Since they had made previous arrangements to have his ashes returned to them for private burial, there was no further business to attend to. Dr. Jameson left them alone then, saying to take as much time as they needed, and to feel free to leave via the back door whenever they were ready. They remained with Codi for some time, hating so much to leave him there.   Eventually they gently removed his collar and gave him one last hug. It was over. "Thank you, Codi," Karen whispered. "Thank you for a job well done. We'll never forget you. Be happy, now. Goodbye dear friend."

For a good part of that day, Karen walked and walked in the rain, hardly aware that she was soaked right through. The cold and discomfort matched her mood. She knew that only time would ease the pain, but for now she accepted the heartache.

Chapter 4: Back at the shelter

After only a few days, Cujo found himself settling in quite nicely at the shelter. In fact, he rather enjoyed the freedom of his large kennel and his daily walks with gentle, caring people. Some of them worked at the shelter and some came in every now and then. The other dogs told him they were called volunteers, and that they came to visit the dogs here just to make them feel loved. Cujo had never known so many people who freely offered such kind words and frequent scratches behind the ears. He was so thankful not to be locked in that small space anymore. He still missed his people, however, especially his kids. But he had come to accept that they wouldn't be taking him home ever again. His heart felt a little sad by this, much as it had felt when he was taken from his mother and his sisters at the farm. It only hurt really bad for a while and then with time, you began to forget. You moved on and learned what was expected of you in your new life. Cujo wondered what his new life would be like after the shelter. Would he find new people in a forever home this time? Someone to love him as much as he wanted to love. Someone he could protect and stand by for all of his days? Cujo knew again, that only time would tell. What he didn't know, was how short a time he really had for that to happen.

Most dogs were only kept at the shelter for a few weeks. And for Cujo the clock had begun ticking down. Lots of people came to the shelter to look for new companions. Once a little girl and her dad took Cujo for a walk and stayed to pet him for quite a while. The little girl was just the kind of friend Cujo would love to have. He would walk by her side, sleep by her bed and take care of her in every way a dog could. He was so hopeful that they would take him home. But in the end, he heard those same human words that he had heard before. "He's just too big." He never saw the little girl again.

For several more long days, there were no visitors that stopped by Cujo's crate. He enjoyed hearing the other dogs bark with happiness as they left with happy new owners; for a dog knows no such thing as envy or jealousy, only joy for the good fortune of others. Maybe soon it would be his turn.

Chapter 5: Moving on

Karen couldn't believe that two weeks had passed since they had lost Codi. She still felt him with her everywhere; in the car, at home, even when she walked down the street. At times, she swore she could hear his nails click clacking across the floor. She would turn, almost expecting to see him there. She still expected to see him standing at the top of the stairs when she finished her day, wagging his tail and waiting patiently for his walk. But she also knew that the pain was growing softer. She could talk about him now without crying, at least. She could laugh with family members about some of the crazy things he had done. She knew she was healing. And she knew that she was starting to miss having a dog around. Will had asked her several times if she was ready to start thinking about another dog, but until now, Karen had been emphatic in her refusal. Until now, it had seemed too soon. It had seemed somehow disloyal to Codi. But Karen was beginning to sense a change. Some little voice was telling her it was time to move on, that maybe there was another dog out there that needed her and the love she had to give. And then she had the dream. It was just her and Codi in the dream. They were walking and playing as they always had, happy and smiling, but there was one big difference. Codi was entirely white. In the dream, Karen seemed oblivious to this fact. She knew only that Codi was running with her like he had as a puppy, tail wagging and short little legs trying to keep up. Karen awoke with such a feeling of contentment and peace. Although she only told close family members about the dream, she believed it was an omen. A sign from Codi that it was time to move on. Maybe today she would suggest to Will that they just go see what dogs were at the shelter. "I don't know for sure, that I'm ready," Karen said. "But let's just go see. I just have a feeling that maybe we are meant to go today." When they arrived at the shelter, they asked about the dogs that were available for adoption. As the girl described several of the dogs, Karen listened but didn't feel like any of them sounded quite right. Until she spoke of one particular rescue. "We do have a dog who was surrendered about two weeks ago," she said as she read from a clipboard of papers. He was left here February 10 by his previous owners. Karen heard very little of her next words, struck by the fact that this dog had been surrendered on the very day that they had had to put Codi down. Karen felt sure that this was the connection she was waiting for. This was the dog they were meant to have. "We would like to see that dog," Karen said. "He sounds perfect!"

Chapter 6: The Connection

The days moved on, and as much as he was comfortable at the shelter, Cujo began to feel very restless. He sensed that something new was coming his way. Then one day he felt an unusual sadness mixed with an odd kind of happiness in his belly. Something was different. He didn't understand what it was or where it was coming from but he knew that it meant there was a change coming for him. Somehow, somewhere the spirit of an unknown comrade was calling to him, telling him that soon, he would find his place and continue some very important work.

Sure enough, later that same day, a middle aged couple came to the shelter. They seemed to walk directly to his crate, bypassing several other dogs that wagged and wiggled and jumped and barked to get their attention. There was a sadness surrounding them, but it was tempered with a glimmer of hope and need. The woman person looked deep into his eyes and Cujo felt an immediate connection. This was the person he was meant to take care of. This was the person that his spirit companion was leading him to. Somehow he had to let her know that they were meant to be together. Since he was in the crate, he couldn't approach her and lean up against her to show his affection, so he did what he could. As she offered her hand through the bars of the crate, he licked it ever so gently, trying to show his love. Cujo watched as a different sensation appeared in the woman's eyes. It was love for sure and Cujo's heart almost burst. The couple left then, and Cujo was worried that they might not return. But the very next day the woman was back. She came alone this time to see him again. She stayed for only a short while but promised him that everything was going to be ok. He was going to be their dog and he was going to have the best life ever.

Sure enough, a few days later, the man person returned and Cujo was led out of his crate and into the care of the friendly, gentle man. He rode in the back seat of the car and he felt so wonderful. He was going to his forever home and he knew it. He could feel the spirit of the dog who had sat right here before him. He could feel all the positive love and energy that filled the air. As soon as he entered the house and met the woman person again, he knew he had absolutely nothing to fear. The spirit of the other dog was still here, waiting to pass the task of caring for his people over to Cujo. Cujo accepted the responsibility eagerly and made a promise to his departed companion that he would be loyal, loving and true to this family for all of his days on this earth. With that, the other spirit moved on and Cujo felt a happiness unlike anything he had ever felt before.

As the days went by, Cujo began to learn the routines and habits of the household. He was no longer called Cujo, but was renamed Riley. His people had smiled and made a joke about him having the "life of Riley." He didn't really know what that meant, but somehow he knew it was good.

And so it was. Riley lived out his life with the couple who had loved and cared for so many other dogs in their time. He continued the work that Codi and the others before him had begun. He was happy and content. He had found his forever home and it would be his until the time came to pass the job along to someone else. He hoped that day was a long way off.

The End

Tales from the Dog Park
(Dog stories as told by Riley)

In "Connected Souls", you were introduced to Cujo, the shelter dog who was adopted and renamed Riley. Riley has been living it up with his loving owners for over 12 years, and is now enjoying his golden years napping on the couch and reflecting on his life experiences. He still visits the local dog park every day where he likes to share his stories with the other dogs who gather there. These are some of those stories.

I am Riley

It's a typical day at the dog park. Dogs of all shapes and sizes are running around, noses to the ground sniffing. I once heard an owner compare this behavior to something humans do called "reading the paper." I guess they think it's how we gather the latest news on the who, what, and where of dog society. At any rate, I have come to the dog park as I do every day, to sniff, greet and to share. But before I begin, let me tell you a bit about myself. I am Riley. Perhaps you met me previously in a book called Connected Souls which is the story my owner wrote about my very beginning time. But in case you haven't met me before, let me say again I am Riley. I am a rescue dog. My owners, Karen and Will took me home from the shelter to give me the "Life of Riley" as they say. I am indeed a blessed dog. I have moved with my people several times and each and every time they included me in all the preparations and decisions.

They made sure each home had a good yard for me and places where I could walk and chase my Frisbee. Every time we moved, my toys, blankets and bed were carefully packed so I would never have to be without them. I am well fed. In fact, my human "Mom", Karen, cooks homemade food for me every day, and bakes the tastiest treats ever!

The town where I currently live has a new dog park where my friends and I can all run free, without the hindrance of leash or collar. It's not a large area by any means, and it is entirely fenced so we are safe from danger. Naturally we would all prefer to run completely free and romp through the woods and fields, but that would surely make our humans anxious. These types of boundaries seem to help them relax while we run free, so we simply accept it as a good thing. We pay little notice to the fence anyway, as there are plenty of great trees to mark, long grass to chomp, and even a pond where we can cool off on hot days. We quite enjoy our daily romps there, and the young fellows always look to me to share dog stories and experiences from my life. I enjoy this, as I believe my wisdom and guidance may help some of the youngsters find their way in the human world a little easier. This book is an account of those stories. Hopefully human friends who read it will gain insight into the hearts and souls of the four legged companions who love them and want for nothing more than to make them happy.

Anyway, back to the dog park.

"Here he comes! Here he comes!" I hear their voices as I saunter towards the gated entry of the park. Before I am through the double gates, I can hear them start.

"Hey Riley! Got any good stories today?" I take a quick inventory of who is present today. My stories are often geared towards who is listening that day. You see, each of my friends is at a different stage of life and needs different things. With a quick read of the crowd, I see Jake, Chase, Max, Brandi and Tucker. Jake is a big black lab about 5 years old and full of endless energy. Chase is a small Sheltie who I often feel is much too vocal. Max is possibly my best friend. He is old, like me, a Shepherd Collie mix whose had some hard times and as a result is pretty aloof. I often have to work at getting him involved in the group. Brandi is a beautiful Golden Retriever. She reminds me of my dog Mom. She is gentle and patient and always listens with genuine interest to all of my stories. And finally, the remaining dog here today is Tucker. I have known Tucker almost all of my life. He was part of the family before I even came along. He visits our house often with his people and we are old pals. His human Mom and mine are sharing stories today too, while we dogs play. When I take a break from socializing with my canine friends, I love to listen to their conversation. They smile and laugh a lot and their happiness envelopes us all.

"Hey, Riley!" It's Jake making all the ruckus. "Got any good stories today?"

"In a minute, friends. A guy's gotta take care of business first." The others continue their sniffing and frolicking while I take my time tending to the usual daily routine. As I come up over the small hill at the back of the park, I see that a newcomer has arrived on the scene. The other dogs have all headed over to say hello and sniff their welcome. They completely encircle this poor creature who is quite obviously a little overwhelmed by all the sudden attention. The crowd spans out a bit as I approach, almost as if they want to give me my own chance to say hello. I smile to myself at the instant respect that old age commands. The new dog is a medium sized mixed breed. By size, smell and behavior I guess

him to be a mix of beagle and blue heeler. He is short legged, with mostly a beagle's markings except for areas where the fur is speckled. His eyes are round and, at the moment somewhat fearful. He looks tense; ready to run at any moment. I hear his owner calling him Boomer and encouraging him to "go play." I think Boomer needs a little help from a friend, so I step up.
"Ok guys. Let's give the little fella a bit of breathing room," I say and they all back away a bit. "New here to the dog park, are you? Well you have nothing to fear. These guys and gals may seem a bit crazy, but they're all friendly. They just get a bit excited when someone new joins the gang." He seems to relax. I urge him to come take a walk around the park with me. Once we have lapped the park and he has sufficiently marked some territory, he begins to relax and interact with the others. He leaves my side now, and goes running after Jake and Brandi with Chance in hot pursuit. Tucker

and Max, the old guys, hang back, as I do, and watch their fun. In our minds I know each one of us is remembering the good old days when we could run like that.

I remember a time too, when I was timid and afraid of the world just like Boomer. And I remember an incident that happened shortly after I came to live with Karen and Will. I can chuckle about it now, but at the time I thought for sure I was a dead dog. Maybe that will be the story for today.

And so our time at the dog park ends as it always does, with all the dogs spread out in the shade of the giant oak tree, listening to the stories that myself or one of the other old guys has to tell, while the owners chat and exchange dog stories of their own on the benches that are scattered throughout the park.

But anyway, like the title says, this book is about stories I tell. So let's get to them, shall we?

The Chase

You wouldn't know it to look at me today, but there was a time when I could run like the wind. There wasn't a dog that could catch me. It's a good thing too, because there was one day when I had to run for my life!

You see, whenever we moved to a new house, Karen and Will always made sure that there were plenty of places where I could go for a free run off leash to get good exercise. Near this house, there was an awesome cornfield with a tractor track that went completely around the field. The farmer was a dog lover and had no problems with dogs running free on the track, as long as we stayed out of the corn field. We dogs were so grateful for a place to run, we made sure never to go off the track. It was a great place to run. The ground was packed down and level so we never had to worry about stumbling into a hole or tripping in soft dirt. Most days Karen took me to the field in the morning, and Karen and Will took me together in the evenings. I really looked forward to those runs. Naturally I could run a lot faster that my owners could walk, so I used to run way up ahead to the bend in the track. Then, because I couldn't see them anymore, I would turn around and run full tilt all the way back to them! It was great fun!

I always had to walk to the field and home again on my leash because there was a busy road to cross, gardens and green lawns to avoid, and small children who were afraid of dogs to pass by. But Karen and Will would always give me as much leash free time as possible. But there was one day that I wished I had been on my leash a little sooner.

We were just coming out from the bottom of the track to head home. Karen and Will were chatting and I knew Will would be clipping my leash on soon. I had wandered over to a particularly interesting patch of long grass. There had been a dog there recently whose scent I didn't recognize and I was trying to get a good read on him. I must have been deep into sniffing because I didn't see or hear the other dog coming until he was right on top of me. I heard the snarl before I saw the face, and that was all it took to make me move. This was not a friend coming to say hello, this was a mean, aggressive fellow, who didn't like any other dogs stepping on what he believed was his turf. I had never been in a dog fight before, and had no desire to be in one now. I had seen other dogs come through the shelter that had survived a fight or two and believe me, it wasn't pretty. Let me tell you, at that moment I was terrified. My first instinct was to run, and that's exactly what I did. I tucked my tail as low between my legs as I could and I turned on all the burners. I could hear Karen and Will's voices calling to me, and I could hear another man's voice calling another dog's name but I wasn't listening, just running. I could sense that I was running a lot faster than my foe, but I didn't slow down. I didn't really even look where I was going. I ran along the sidewalk so I could avoid the dangerous road, but I had no escape route in mind. I just kept going.

Suddenly something smelled and felt familiar. Home! It hadn't been our home for very long yet, but it had been long enough for me to recognize it. I made a beeline straight for the front porch, certain that I would be safe there. Finally, panting and exhausted, I stopped and sat on the top step. I knew no dog, no matter how vicious, would dare to attach me on my owner's property. I didn't need to worry, however, as I soon caught sight of my attacker secured on the leash of his man. The man was talking to Will and yanking hard on the dog's leash. Karen was hurrying towards me, looking worried and scared. It wasn't until I saw her expression that I thought about the risks I had taken crossing the busy road. I hadn't even thought about cars, or the danger they represented, all I wanted to do was get home.

In an instant Karen was on the step with me, hugging my neck and scratching my ears and telling me what a good dog I was to run home. Seems she was afraid I would just keep running, that she might never see me again. I realized then, how unsure they were that I loved them and trusted them. It was true that when they first brought me home, I had trust issues. After all, my first humans had been very mean to me. But I know love when I see it, and I knew these people loved me. And I think they know now, after today, that I love them. I proved to them that my place is with them and that anyplace where we all live together is home.

Frisbees

I realized a very strange thing at the dog park today. Just on the other side of our fence, there is an odd looking structure that humans play with. It is made of metal and chains and I've heard it referred to as a Frisbee golf basket. Apparently this is some type of game that humans play where they throw Frisbees into this basket.

Now, I suppose, for humans this makes the game of Frisbee a bit more interesting, and that's all well and good. But what I can't understand, is why in the world they would build a Frisbee game for people right beside a park where dogs come to run and play. Don't they realize that all those Frisbees flying by on the other side of the fence creates pure torture for some of us? After all, if you're a Frisbee catching dog and you see Frisbees flying by, the only thing you want to do is catch them, right? It just makes sense! So some of my friends end up running up and down the edge of the dog park looking like dogs gone mad, running and barking and snapping at thin air. It keeps them busy I suppose, and certainly gets them their exercise, but for some, it's pretty annoying.

On the other hand, as far as the humans are concerned, it can sure be a little frustrating for players who have less than perfect aim too, because many of their Frisbees end up in the dog park. Now there are three pretty good reasons why this becomes a problem. One, if you don't happen to be a dog lover, you may be a little hesitant to head into a park that's full of free running dogs. And two, even if you love dogs a lot, you might not want to go chasing after some eighty pound lab who has claimed your Frisbee as his own. And three, maybe you don't really want your expensive game quality Frisbee embellished with dozens of tiny tooth marks, cause I'm pretty sure they won't help it to fly better!

At least the organizers of this strange activity had the foresight to put a gate from one area into the other so stray and captured Frisbees could, at least, be reclaimed.

It also put the idea of training Frisbee dogs into the head of many a dog owner who probably should have chosen a much different dog activity.

This was especially true of one of my park buddies, an energetic Aussie named Pete who was in no way quick enough, either in mind or body to be a good disc catcher. Time after time his owner would throw the disc. Time after time, Pete would watch it go sailing by over his head and then run to try and catch it. Needless to say, every time the disc would come down and Pete would either get hit on the head by it, trip over it or run clear on by it. Of course, he did always grab it in the end, and head back to his owner. But even then, he would stop several feet away and drop it, looking expectantly at his owner. Exasperated, his owner would urge him to at least bring it all the way back to him. They continued at this for several days with little progress. Then one day Pete arrived at the park with his lady human instead of the man. She was much more interested in socializing with the other owners and had no interest in playing catch. Pete, I guess, decided this would be a good time to ask the "old pro" how it was really done.

"Hey Riley!" "Can you give me a few pointers? I'd really like to do this thing for my owner. It seems to mean a lot to him."

"Why not?" I thought. "Might as well help the pup out a bit of I can. I was pretty good at it, even if I do say so myself. Mind you, I've had a lot of practice. Will started throwing them for me right from the beginning of our time together. At first he threw them only a short distance so I could get the idea, and then before long I was snatching them out of the air as far as he could throw them. It was a rare thing for me to miss one! But let me tell you, there is some technique to be learned if you want to do it right. So listen up, kiddo, and I'll give you some tips."

I have to hand it to the kid. He really paid attention. And from what I've seen lately, he's put it all into practice. On any given day now, you can catch a very exuberant Pete and a very proud man playing Frisbee catch together and loving every minute of it.

But that's how we dogs are. It's just in our nature to please our people and do whatever they expect from us. The real bonus comes when that something is a thing that we both enjoy and that strengthens the bond we share.

"Way to go, Pete!" "You do us all proud!"

Scary Things

It seems there are a few holidays every year where humans feel compelled to light up the sky with loud, scary lights that scare the fur off every dog I know. They call them "fireworks," and I have no idea what the attraction is. Some of them included really loud bangs and brilliant flashes of light. Some were a single flash followed by a sound I called the "zipper'" It made me feel as though some giant dog devouring creature was going to descend from the sky and carry me away.

For most of us animals, anything that has anything at all to do with fire is something to be avoided at all costs. Unless of course, it involves a cozy fireplace with a nice soft rug in front! Even then, we respect this fire and are prepared to take flight at any moment in case that fire escapes its place. But these exploding, blazing sky fires are something we simply can't accept.

Now some of you young fellows want to know how I deal with these things. Fortunately for me, my people have realized how upsetting these events are for me, and they leave me at home whenever they go to see them. If your people haven't quite got that message yet, be patient. They will learn. Soon they will realize that your trembling bones, and racing heart are for real and they'll leave you at home too. If, for some reason, these events take place within your own territory, and you can't avoid them, here are some hints to help you through.

Find a hiding place as far away from the noise as possible. For me, this usually meant heading down to the basement. I found a dark little corner under an old workbench that made the sounds almost impossible to hear, and there were no windows so I couldn't hear anything. So check around your house and see if you can find a place like that. But having said that, you should also know that these crazy things are usually short-lived. I've never seen any last more than a few minutes, even though it seems like a lifetime when you're a dog! And as scary as they may be, you aren't really in any danger. That's really all I have to say about fireworks. But thunderstorms, now that's a dog of another color!

I hate to admit it, being the old wise man that I am, but I am still afraid of thunderstorms. Even though these old tired ears hear very little of them anymore, there is still something heavy and frightening in the air that sets my every nerve on edge. And the lightening! It's more frightening than anything. The flashes are so bright and shoot down from the sky as if the world is going to end. I sense fear and anxiety in my people too, and that makes me even more afraid. My every instinct tells me to go to them and help them feel less afraid, and yet, my own soul is so terrified that all I want to do is run and hide. In the end, I just wind up pacing around the house until the whole thing is over. I usually find a dark spot not far from where my people are, and I go from there to them and back again. I have had several good friends over the years who have offered suggestions for overcoming their fear of storms, but none of them ever worked for me.

One fine chap, a Golden named Branson, used to wear quite a funny looking blanket that his folks called a storm coat. It was supposed to eliminate that scary feeling that fills the air, but my people somehow never got wind of this invention. It didn't look all that comfortable anyway.

Another friend, an old mongrel named Lad used to hide outside under the cars. I suppose maybe he felt safe there, but let me tell you, he didn't stay dry and I'm sure he could still hear all the thunder!

So, I'm sorry to say, friends that thunderstorms are just a part of life to be endured. With any luck, you'll only experience them once in a while. Trust in your people to take care of you and you'll be fine. Stick together always, for that is where your strength lies.

Rabbits and Groundhogs

Everyone always talks about dogs chasing cats. Well, I for one, have never bothered to chase cats. For one thing, I simply don't like their attitude, and for another, there are so many of them around, they are just simply of no interest to me. But show me a rabbit or a groundhog, and its game on! Both of these creatures are fast and whenever our paths cross, it's like the green flag waving at a car race. I'm ready to chase them and they're ready to run.

At the house where we used to live, there was a place we all called the meadow. Like I said before, my people always made sure there was a place for me to run free wherever we lived, and this house was no exception. There wasn't a real "dog Park" like there was in the big city, but it was a spot where everyone who lived nearby brought their dogs. I think it was just a part of an old abandoned farm field but it sure was a great place to play.

We weren't the only ones there, though. It was also the place that several groundhog families called home. Now these weren't just your everyday groundhogs, either. I'm pretty sure they were fans of the game I've heard of called "Whack-a-Mole." These crafty little devils would pop up out of their holes just high enough and long enough to catch our attention and then once we got close they'd duck down out of sight and leave us standing in the middle of the field looking all of lost and confused, like some kind of simpletons. After a while we caught on to their tricks but we never stopped chasing them. We liked to get all the new pups in the meadow to chase them too, so we older guys could sit back and have a good snicker at their foolish antics. Oh, the joys of being an old dog!

Rabbits galore lived in this field as well. We chased them on occasion, too, but they didn't see it as a game quite like the groundhogs did. When we came upon a rabbit, they seemed to be genuinely afraid of us. I suppose that's because there are some of our kind who do chase and catch rabbits, just out of instinct. As for myself, I was purely curious about the little fellows. I wouldn't dream of ever hurting one, but I always thought they would offer up a great game of tag if they just had a little more trust. I often hear my people laughing and telling others about my foiled attempts to initiate a game of chase with a local family of rabbits.

I was trotting along, nose to the ground, when I suddenly came upon a rabbit hole. I stuck my nose in and had a long sniff. There was definitely somebody home! I drew back and waited by the hole. Sure enough, within a few seconds, a large rabbit stuck his head out. I jumped up, he took a look at me, and headed back down! This happened several times. Up, down. Up, down. I couldn't figure out what kind of game this was, but it kept me occupied for some time. Turns out, that was his game plan all along! While I was busy playing pop up with him, his family of little ones was escaping to safety out the back door. Karen and Will had been watching this whole comedy unfold and were quite amused. Of course, I had to act like I knew what had been going on all along so as not to lose any respect from the gang. Truth was, I had to give those rabbits a lot of credit. Pretty smart fellows, I'd say!

One day a rabbit and I had a great game of chase in our back yard. One morning when Karen first put me out, there was a small rabbit munching happily away on some plants in our garden. I was just a pup still, and I ran over to say hi, thinking he would want to play. As soon as he saw me he scooted to the fence without even so much as a sniff in my direction. Thinking he wanted to play tag, I chased after him. He beat me to the fence then turned and shot back across the lawn. Of course, for me, across the lawn was only a few strides, but my bunny friend was running his little legs off. We continued that game for some time. Up to the edge of the fence and back. Up to the fence and back. I was just deciding that this game was getting a bit boring when on one trip to the fence he suddenly disappeared through a little gap. He took off into the forest leaving me panting after him at the fence. Seems he wasn't playing tag with me after all, but was searching frantically for that escape route! Oh well, it was fun while it lasted!

Criminal Dog

Believe it or not, I have a criminal record. I'm not an aggressive dog by any means, but the laws in the city can often work against us when people fail to be a little understanding. Let me tell you about the one time I got Karen into big trouble with the courts.

We had all gone for a run at the dog park as we often do on sunny days. The three of us, myself, Tucker and Pirate, another family dog were all in the back of our SUV. We pulled into Tucker's driveway and got ready to jump out. The adults were busy getting all the kids out of the car and into the house so they just opened the back door and let us out. Just as the last of us got all fours on the ground, a lady appeared from around the corner of the fence walking her little sheltie. When he spied the lot of us he began tugging on his leash and barking, which naturally drew our attention. Since he was barking a big hello, we barked back and all ran over to greet him. I guess to his owner this seemed like an attack. Quick as a wink she snatched her little guy up into her arms and headed for home. Disappointed that we couldn't say hello, we all retreated into the house. Little did we know that she had been terrified by our approach and had called the police to report us as vicious and out of control. Later that evening, an agent from the humane society, accompanied by a policeman came to Tucker's door to give him a ticket for being "at large" which I guess means running loose. On the following days, Pirate and I also received tickets from the humane society. Karen was really upset by this, claiming that we were on our own property and had not in fact done anything wrong. To her, and to all of us, it seemed just like one big over reaction by a very nervous lady. Kind of a "her word against ours" situation. After all, her dog started barking first. And all we wanted to do was say hello. But laws are laws, say the humans who write them, and technically we were off leash where we weren't allowed to be.

Even though Karen took the issue to court, stating that we were actually on private property and under complete control, she still had to pay the fine. That was my second strike. My first was much less traumatic for everyone, but it got put on my record just the same.

It all happened when I was still a very new adopted dog, a puppy still, and very nervous around everyone. Karen and Will had taken me out for a walk on my leash and had stopped to talk to some neighbors. Their little guy was buzzing all around us on a three wheeled riding thing called a "big wheel." It was low to the ground, and he kept zipping past my back end where I couldn't see what he was doing. I was getting really scared by the speed and the noise of the wheeled thing right behind me. One time he came just a little too close and I snapped my head around and snarled a warning. I had no intention of hurting him and I certainly didn't mean to bite him. But just as I snarled, he came a little too close, and I nipped his leg. He squealed and ran to his people. Will pulled me in closer on my lead and scolded me a bit, then made sure the little guy was ok. It seemed like a pretty superficial wound.

We continued on our walk, thinking the incident was forgotten, until a knock came to our door the next morning. Seems the boy's folks took him to the hospital to make sure the wound didn't require stitches. When they reported it as a dog bite, they had to tell them about me. Now there was an officer at our door making sure I had had all my shots and that I wasn't going to be a danger to anyone.

Will explained the whole situation, and I was given the ok to stay home. For a wee minute there though, I was really scared. I thought for sure I was headed back to the shelter once again. I've heard humans say something about three strikes and you're out. Well I'm not entirely sure what that means, or where you go when you're out but I know I don't want to find out! I had two strikes against me and that was enough!

Will must have read the fear in my eyes because after the agent left, he gave me a big hug around my neck, and told me not to worry. He said I was their dog now and nobody was ever going to take me away again. I gave him a very grateful lick, and vowed to trust that Will and Karen would keep me safe; even from wild kids and noisy wheeled contraptions.

Bakery Dog

This will be a short chapter from the story of my life but it was full of good times so it is worth a mention. You see, for a while I was a business dog. Now, I wasn't the CEO of the company or anything, but I was the CTT. This stands for Chief Taste Tester. You see, Karen and Will owned a dog bakery. It was named after me and my cousin Tucker. It was called Tucker O'Riley's Dog Bakery. Let me tell you, it was a grand place for a dog to spend his days. Every day Karen baked fresh treats and dog food for her customers. There was every kind of dog treat you could imagine. There were cheese treats, chicken treats, bacon treats, birthday cakes, frozen doggie yogurt and tons of other tasty stuff.

Of course, it was my job to make sure everything met Karen's high quality standards before they hit the shelves. I can hear your drool hitting the floor! Ya, it was a tough job but some dog had to do it!

Karen was always careful not to feed me too many treats though. She was always looking out for my health!

The dog bakery was a neat place to socialize too. You see, Karen allowed, even encouraged, her customers to bring their dogs into the bakery. I got to know some of the regulars pretty well and we had some good times together. Holidays were always the best. We had special events for Christmas and Halloween. At Christmas the dogs came in and helped their owners fill a stocking full of special treats. Everyone did a lot of gift shopping too so the shop was full of extra awesome squeaky toys and stuffies. There was such excitement in the air. It really made me feel good.

At Halloween believe it or not, we actually had costume parties! Now, I think these were definitely more for the benefit of the humans than the dogs. I mean, what dog really wants to parade around in a fireman's jacket or a pair of fairy wings? Well, I suppose some of the tiny little fluff balls that came in the bakery didn't mind, but it was sure painful for some of us bigger guys and gals. But, we love to please our masters, so we do it, right? And really, isn't it worth wearing some goofy get up if it means a few extra yummy treats?

We even played games at these events. Maybe you've heard of people bobbing for apples? Well we canine creatures like to bob for hot dogs! Go figure!!!!

Anyway, Karen ran the dog bakery for a few years and then it was time for us to move on again, so it was closed down. I must say, I was sad to see it go. Those were some good times. But all was not lost. Karen continued to cook the same yummy homemade food for me, and she still bakes fresh treats every week. No store bought milk bones for this guy! But listen up, friends. If you're ever on a road trip with your folks and you pass a sign for a dog bakery, make sure you get the word across that you want to stop in. I hear they are springing up all over the country, and they are well worth the visit!

Life in the Woods

Well we have moved once again. This time, we are living in the country so there is no longer the need to find leash free parks for this dog! Here I have three acres of my own woods to explore. There is a cool hiking trail right out our back door that Karen and I walk every day, morning and night. There are so many smells out there I never have time to sniff them all. Some of them get my neck hairs in a buzz but most of them are just interesting. I stay clear of ones that smell like skunk or bear, but I am curious about most of the others like deer, moose and chipmunks. I haven't encountered many of them face to face but I know they're there.

One night I felt a low growl just start all by itself in my throat. I felt a real need to warn my folks that something was not quite right outside. Will opened the door and I pushed myself against his leg trying to warn him to stay inside. He got out one of those fancy lights that shine from his hands and pointed it into the backyard. Sure enough, my fears were right. Right at the edge of our deck stood a black bear trying to get the bird seed Karen had left in the storage box. He had torn the lid right off and had the bag of seed in his teeth. Will banged on the door and the bear took his prize and ran off into the woods. No harm came to anyone, but I was on alert for the rest of the night, and the next day when we walked the trail. But I guess Mr. Bear had satisfied himself with his bird seed and had moved on. I know he is never very far away though because I can still sniff his scent. I keep my bear alert growl ready all the time just in case!

One of the other smells I have come to know is Moose. They are some big, let me say, and not an animal I want to get very close to. They don't ever come too close to the house, though, and they don't really represent a danger to my owners. I smell them around now and then but they pretty much go their way and let the rest of the world go by.

One other slight annoyance is the flies. There seems to be an abundance of these in the woods. First come the black flies in late May. They are tiny, pesky little devils that get in my ears and try to feast. Karen has a special spray that she douses me with. Trouble is, I don't much like the smell or the feel of the spray, but it beats getting all chewed up! Deer flies and horse flies are a nuisance too. They aren't nearly as stealth as the black flies. In fact, they're about as bold as it gets. They buzz all around my head and land right on my nose! I try to brush them off with my paws but sometimes they take a chunk out of me first! The big secret with those guys is to keep moving. They seem to have trouble getting a good hold on a moving target. But if you want to take in an afternoon snooze, it's best to do it inside!

All in all, I enjoy being a country dog. It is different than living in the city for sure. It's a lot quieter for one thing, and I don't have to worry about busy roads. I never have to be tied up or leashed and the freedom is absolutely wonderful. I have lots of spots where I can dig big holes if the urge strikes me, and there is a small stream I can muck around in to cool off. The water tastes pretty good too! There's tons of space to play Frisbee and more sticks just laying around than any dog could ever catch or chew. And the grass! This country place has lots of grass for munching. Now I don't know about all dogs, but I can tell you, there are few things in this world more tasty than a fresh young shoot of grass that's covered in morning dew. That is a treat to be savored! Yep, living in the country has been a blast. Or at least it was until last spring. That's when my life changed a lot.

Stink Eye

I am a one eyed dog. When people say I'm giving them the evil eye, or the stink eye, as they sometimes say, it is really the evil _eye_! I used to have two eyes but one day last spring I did a rather foolish thing and now I am forever more a one eyed dog.

It was middle of March, a beautiful spring day. There was still a lot of snow on the ground but it was starting to melt. It was hard knowing where to step to keep from sinking up to your belly. I'm getting on, you know, and dragging my hind end up out a snow drift is pretty hard work. This day, I should have been a little more careful where I walked.

I had been laying quietly enjoying some nice spring sunshine on a dry bit of deck when all of a sudden a group of chipmunks began to chatter. They were chasing each other all over the yard and making one mighty racket! At first I tried to ignore them, but then my chasing bug got the better of me and I took off after them. All caught up in the chase, I didn't pay attention to where I was going. I ran up onto what I thought was a pile of snow. Next thing I knew, the snow gave way and I was plunged into a pile of brush that had been buried. There was a lot of snapping and cracking and then all I remember is a lot of pain. I suddenly couldn't see out of one eye and my head felt like someone was jabbing me with a giant needle. I remember yelping and running for all I was worth to get away from whatever it was that was attacking me. Eventually I heard Karen's voice coming to me through my fog of pain. I knew I had to go back to her for help. I followed her voice and found my way back. By this time the pain was dulling a bit, but I still couldn't see very well. I was panting like a locomotive, and my heart was still racing. Karen brought me inside and calmed me down. Karen made an emergency appointment for me and the doctor gave her lots of medicine. For the next couple of weeks I had to endure eye drops twice a day, and great big pills that Karen tried to disguise in slices of cheese. Karen thought she was pulling the wool over my eyes, but I'm too smart for that. I never let on that I knew the pills were in there. After all, cheese is one of my most favorite treats. As hard as it was, I tried my best to be a brave dog and take my medicine willingly. I could tell how sad it made Karen feel to have to give it to me, especially the eye drops. She would always say she was sorry. I wanted to make her feel better, tell her it wasn't her fault, and the only way I could do that was to take it all like the big dog I am.

By this time, the pain in my eye had become something like a dull, always just kind of there, headache. I could endure it, but I never felt really normal. I couldn't see anything out of my damaged eye, either, so life was a bit unpleasant. After several check-ups, the doctor told Karen and Will that my eye was not going to get any better. If they left the eye alone, it meant I would have chronic pain for the rest of my days, and there was also the risk of infection from the deceased eye. The alternative was to remove the eye. And because the doctor said that was the best choice for my health, that is what Will and Karen decided to do.

I remember the day we left the hospital after getting that news. I could tell Karen was feeling really down about it. I didn't know how to make her feel better so I just stayed real close by and sent her lots of dog love with my good eye. I was really wishing there was some way that I could tell her that life with one eye would be just fine. How frustrating not to have human language! Turns out, there was someone else who was going to pass that information along for me. We stopped at one of my favorite parks on the way home, and I will be eternally grateful that we did. As we pulled to a stop in the parking lot, a dog that was there with his owner came running over to the car waiting for me to get out and say hello. Karen was hesitant to let me out afraid that I was not yet up to playing with a rambunctious friend. As Karen got out of the car, the other lady apologized for her dog being so bold. Karen said it wasn't a problem, but that she just wasn't sure how much I would feel like playing. As Karen explained my condition, and the news we had just received, the other lady smiled and said that she'd like us to meet someone. She called over another of her dogs that was standing nearby. As he got closer, Karen and I realized that this fellow had no eyes! His owner explained how they had both been removed due to disease, and that he was living a happy, productive life even though blind. Karen and the woman chatted for a bit, and the blind dog and I got acquainted. By the end of our visit I knew

Karen was feeling a lot better. I guess sometimes good things just happen when you really need them to!

The appointment for surgery was made for the following week. I felt really bad because the day they chose was Karen's birthday. She should have been out celebrating and having a good time. Instead she was sitting at home worrying about me. Anyway, it all went well and I was back home in my own bed by suppertime. I was so sleepy from all the drugs that I just slept for hours. By the next day I was feeling much better. Within a week my stitches had come out and I was free of pain and the headache that had been there since the accident was gone. I had to adjust to seeing with one eye, but that didn't take long. I still bump into things from time to time if I turn too quickly on my blind side, but all in all, I've done very well. One thing I do know for sure is, I

won't go chasing any goofy chipmunks
through the snow!

Senior Dog

Well it's been a year now since I became a one eyed dog. That happened when I was 11, and I have started to slow down a bit now. Life is a little harder with one eye, but I am still loved and cared for and give back as much love as I can. My ears have stopped working as they should, and I sometimes have trouble hearing what people are saying. I know Karen still smiles and gestures when we are heading out for walks or rides in the car, and I still understand that. I know that I don't always hear people when they call to me, and quite often people reach out and pet me before I even know they are close by. I get startled sometimes but I always know as long as I am with the people who love me, that I am safe.

I can't hear the chipmunks much anymore so there is less temptation to go chasing them. I'm also happily oblivious to most crashes and bangs of thunder. I still feel the air change when there is a storm, and I still get freaked out by the lightening, but the rumbling rolls of thunder that used to set my nerves on edge no longer bother me. Thank goodness for small mercies!

One thing I'm not any too happy about is the stiffness I am beginning to feel in my back end. It's such as effort now to get up after I've been napping. I don't run much anymore either. Try as I might, I just can't get these old legs going. I have given up chasing sticks and my Frisbees have all been retired to the toy box. They now form the substance of my dreams. Just stop by sometime and you'll find me blissfully napping with legs, eyes and jowls twitching in delight as I relive the antics of my youth. I can't jump up onto the beds anymore, and that is really something I miss. There's just nothing like pulling all the covers that smell like your people into one big pile and snuggling in! But I can still make it up onto the couch, so I'm good there. I have my own thick bed, too, when I want it.

Getting in and out of the car is a challenge, but amazingly enough, there is always someone there to heft my mighty back end up if I need help. Road trips are still the best fun of all and I don't want to ever have to miss them! I sleep more now, but that is a privilege of the old in any species, and I take full advantage of my position.

All in all, I have had a good life. Even though things were a bit rocky in the beginning, and I will not likely ever completely forget those days, I have forgiven the people who gave me my first home. They did their best to love me, but ours just wasn't a good match. I am thankful that they had the kindness to take me where there was an opportunity for me to find new people to love me. I know it was probably hard for them to admit their failure as it was hard for me to admit that my love was not enough for them. But we have all moved on. I hope they have found a dog that is right for them because everyone should experience the kind of love that only a dog can give.

As for me, I will be forever grateful to Karen and Will, and to Codi, whose soul I believe is what brought us together. From that first day when I licked Karen's hand, to the final moment in the future when we look into each other's eyes for the last time, I will feel forever loved.

Back at the Park

I can hear the ruckus before I even get to the gate. "Here he comes! Riley is here! It's story time!" I pick up the pace a little, just to show that I can, ignoring the stiff hip joints that protest my vanity. I lift my head and wag my tail high. These young pups can really use a mentor to help them learn the ropes. That is my purpose, my aspiration. As I approach the gang, I study the crowd and decide what story I will tell today. Will it be a tale of courage and bravery? A tale of calamity and humor? Or maybe something a bit more touching for the girls. After all, even an old dog like me still likes to impress the ladies! Whatever story it ends up being, I know it will be good. For all my life has been good. I am a blessed dog, but right now, my audience awaits.

The end

Bear
©Dana Landers 2012

Chapter One

Lisa stood at the picture window watching Mother Nature deliver yet another wintery blast. It was nearly the middle of April and the last thing she wanted to see was more snow. Just last week she had been thrilled to see her first robin bobbing around in the odd patch of overwintered grass that fought desperately for the warmth of a little sun. Even the crocuses had begun to show their tiny purple and yellow faces. Now they looked more like the leftovers of last night's wilted salad.

Her hand rested on the large furry head of the big black dog at her side. His posture matched hers exactly although she was pretty sure he couldn't really see much as he looked outside with her. Nor could he hear the roar of the icy north wind that whipped the snow almost completely sideways. Bear had just celebrated his thirteenth birthday and this winter was taking a heavy toll. His once beautiful brown eyes were clouded with cataracts now and his hearing had been gone for some time. He had learned to cope amazingly well and compensated for the loss of those two senses with an extremely keen sense of smell and touch. Lisa knew that this might very well be Bear's last winter, and the thought of losing him squeezed her heart like a vice, and although she knew his leaving her was inevitable, she didn't want him to go during the winter. There was no rational explanation for this desire; she just knew that she wanted him to see green grass and sunshine one last time, as though that in itself might make his passing easier.

"Please hang in there, big fella," she said, absently rubbing his head. "You just need to have faith that spring will come again, just like those poor robins out there in the snow. They know. They believe, and you have to too."

Although he couldn't hear her voice, Bear responded readily to her touch, and rubbed his big head against her leg as he leaned his full one hundred and five pounds against her. If he could have his way, he would stay with her forever, but that is not how it goes in the canine world. His time was coming, and he knew these days were precious. He also knew that Lisa would let him go when the time finally came. He trusted her completely and loved her unconditionally.

And that is why, on this wintery day, and every day, he stood by her side. He would walk with her today and brave the wind and snow, and God willing, he would walk with her again when the sun warmed the frozen earth and the air filled with scents of a new spring.

Suddenly he sensed her moving away, and he turned towards her, trying to sense her intentions. He could feel her movements and the direction from which they came told him she was preparing to go outside. He sat back on his haunches and waited patiently.

"Well, if we're going out, we better go now," Lisa spoke as though Bear could hear. "It's not going to get any better out there." Although she could have simply opened the door and let the dog out on his own, she never did. She was always afraid that he would wander off and not be able to find his way back. The property that she and her husband Tom owned was bordered by fairly dense woods. Their rustic log home sat in a clearing of almost an acre but she still worried that Bear might stray away from the clearing and become disoriented.

In his younger days, they would often head off into the woods, following the well-worn trail that looped in among the lodge pole pines before winding its way back to the house. Bear would never stay on the trail once he caught the scent of a chipmunk or rabbit, but he never went far from his people either. These days, she was not so sure he could navigate even those once familiar trails so well. And so they always ventured out together. In weather like this, they stayed on the shoveled walkways and the long winding drive that a local businessman kept clear for them. Tom worked long hours away from home, often travelling out of town and snow removal was not something Lisa could handle on her own, especially this year when she was five months pregnant. She was thankful for this arrangement, as she and Bear prepared to head out. If it wasn't for Steve's Snow Removal Service, she would be housebound much of the time. Lisa began layering her outerwear, watching Bear waiting at her side.

 "Bet you wish I could just walk out the door like you do," she joked out loud. "But I don't happen to wear a permanent fur coat and have fuzzy fur between my toes, so you just have to be patient." She pulled on one glove, and left the other hand bare to turn the door knob. She opened the door and

Bear was out before she could take a step. Once he was clear of the doorway, she reached for the inside door to pull it closed. Just as it closed, she heard the distinctive chime of her IPad indicating that she had received an instant message. Thinking that it might be Tom letting her know his flight information, she turned and headed back inside.

"Wait right there, Bear," she called over her shoulder. "I'll be right out." She twisted the knob and pushed the door inward hurrying to reach the IPad on the coffee table just inside. She wanted to catch Tom and chat with him before he boarded the plane. Giving the door a shove behind her, she stepped off the entry way carpet onto the laminate floor of the living room, boots and all. Wet snow had already clumped on the bottom of her boots, and as she stepped onto the slippery floor, her feet came completely out from under her. She slipped backwards, grasping at the air to regain her foothold but landed squarely on her backside with a thump. A searing pain shot through her abdomen and travelled across her back followed by a sudden rush of nausea. For a second or two, Lisa couldn't move. Blackness threatened to overtake her, and the room began a slow spin.

"I have to get help. The baby needs help." Lisa struggled to stay conscious as she crawled towards the table. The IPad had ceased its cheerful blip, and her next thought was of Tom. She pulled herself over to the table and reached for her cell phone. She dialed 911 and then the world went black.

"Hello, do you need help? Hello, what is the nature of your emergency? Hello?" The voice of the 911 dispatcher called into the silent living room. After getting no response the operator immediately went to work to trace the origin of the call. "We have an emergency call on an open cell line. Getting the address now," she reported to the paramedics waiting for her instructions. "Call is coming from a house at 6751 Wyndemere Lane in Clarkesville. Caller has not responded but the line is open."

"On our way," the driver replied.

Bear sat on the porch waiting. He was pretty sure he had felt Lisa come outside, but suddenly he could no longer sense her movements. Her scent was in the air so he thought perhaps she had already moved ahead of him. He slowly brought his old haunches to a standing position and headed off down the lane, trusting that Lisa was somewhere nearby. After a few minutes, Bear noticed that the path was no longer smooth and packed down. Where he was walking now, there were patches of snow that were deeper and crunchy on top. It sliced at his paws with each step and coated the underside of his belly. He could still smell Lisa though, so he kept on walking. She had to be here somewhere. Every few steps, he would stop and sniff the air. Her scent was still around him, but it was growing fainter. He soon realized that Lisa had not headed in this direction, and he knew he needed to find his way back onto the smooth path. With only his sense of smell to guide him, Bear turned and headed back in the opposite direction. He had to find Lisa, or at least his way back to the house. Icy cold wind blew snow into his face that froze onto his fur. His unseeing eyes blinked rapidly to keep the ice away, and his unhearing ears strained to hear some familiar sound. Lisa's scent was even fainter now, and the smells of home were fading fast. The trails and woods that he normally knew so well were void of identifying scents, all diluted by this latest onslaught of winter. His instincts told him to keep moving ahead, and so he did. The wailing sounds of emergency vehicles approaching might have helped him find his way home had he been able to hear them.

Chapter Two

Lisa opened her eyes and struggled to make her fuzzy brain focus on her surroundings. Where was she? Where was Bear? The last thing she remembered was the two of them heading out the door. The room was dark and quiet but she could sense a presence beside her. Turning her head slightly she could see the outline of someone in the chair beside her bed. "Tom?" she whispered, her throat dry and her mouth feeling like gravel.

"Lisa?" Tom bolted upright in the chair and gently took her hand that was free of medical apparatus. "I'm right here. How are you feeling?"

"What happened? Where am I? Where is Bear?" And then it all came flooding back. She gripped Tom's hand in a vice like squeeze. "What about the baby? The baby, Tom! Is the baby okay?" Panic threatened to take her into the darkness again.

Tom gently ran his hand along her cheek and tried to hold her and give her comfort. "The baby is fine...just fine. The doctors gave you something to prevent labor from starting, and everything is back to normal. The baby's vital signs are all good. You just need to rest and relax."

Lisa sank back into the hospital pillows at her back, breathing a long sigh of relief. She rubbed her hand across her belly and was rewarded with a reassuring kick. She smiled. "I can tell," she said softly, taking Tom's hand and placing it over hers. "He's telling me that everything is ok."

"You gave me quite a scare," Tom said. "Not exactly the welcome home I was planning on! There's nothing quite like getting a call from the police while you're stuck at the airport ,standing in a huge long custom's line to get your adrenalin flowing! All they told me was that you'd had an accident and were already here at St. Mike's." Lisa squeezed his hand and smiled weakly.

"I'm sorry," she said. "I really didn't have any control over that part of it." Suddenly her smile disappeared, replaced by a look of sheer panic. "Bear!" she said grabbing Tom's hand. "Where is Bear?"

Tom looked at her, confused. "I came straight from the airport. As far as I know Bear is at home."

"No, No. I mean I don't know!" Lisa shook her head, trying to clear her thoughts. "He was outside already! We were going to go for a walk. Then I heard my IPad chime and I assumed it was you. I wanted to catch you before you got on the plane. Bear was waiting for me outside. Then I fell. I remember calling 911. Bear was still outside! He was alone and outside in the storm! What if the paramedics didn't see him? What if he's still out there waiting for me? In this weather he'll freeze. You have to go and find out. Find out if the paramedics put him inside. Please, Tom. You have to find out!"

Tom took her shoulders and gently pushed her back into the bed. He didn't like the way all the color had drained from her face. This couldn't be good for her or the baby!

"Please, honey, you need to relax. We have to think about the baby. Just rest and I'll go see what I can find out." Lisa nodded and closed her eyes as tears made their way slowly down her cheeks. Tom squeezed her hand and promised to return with any news as quickly as he could.

The nurse at the station told him his best bet would be to try the desk in the emergency room. They would know which paramedics had brought Lisa in. With a growing worry gnawing at him, Tom headed down the hall to the ER. The nurse at the desk remembered him, and the case, but the paramedics that had brought Lisa in several hours before had long since departed.

"Let me get hold of dispatch, and we'll see if we can reach them." She dialed a number into her desk phone and quickly asked for the information she needed. After a short pause, she placed her hand over the mouthpiece and turned to Tom. "They are checking now with those drivers. It should just take a minute or two." Tom nodded and tried to smile. He couldn't imagine what would happen if Bear was lost. Lisa would be devastated, and he didn't know how that might affect the baby on top of what had already happened. "Sir?" the nurse's voice broke through his thoughts. "The paramedics who transported your wife say they didn't see a dog anywhere around." Tom's small glimmer of hope vanished.

"Thank you for your help," he said as he turned to head back to Lisa's room. His heart wrenched at the thought of having to tell her about Bear. And although he didn't want to show his concern, he too was extremely afraid of what the consequences of the situation might be. Even though the snow had stopped, a freezing rain was now beginning to fall. That meant that the temperature was warming up, but ice could be far more treacherous for an old blind dog. Tom hoped with all his heart that Bear had just curled up near the house somewhere to wait for someone to come to him. There were several places on the property that might afford him some protection. "Please, Bear," he thought to himself. "Please be safe." Tom tried to force a happier expression as he entered Lisa's room. Her face looked so pale against the stark whiteness of the bleached hospital sheets. It would break her heart if anything happened to that old dog.

Bear and Lisa had been through a lot together, and he meant the world to her. Bear had been in Lisa's life long before Tom had arrived on the scene, and there were even times, early in their relationship when he secretly wondered if he could ever be first in Lisa's heart. He felt so silly at times being jealous of a dog, and none of Lisa's reassurances could completely dispel his silly notions. In time though, he had come to love Bear almost as much as Lisa did, and as their relationship developed, he quickly learned what it was like to completely love an animal, and he understood.

"Honey," Tom said softly as he perched gently on the side of the bed. Lisa opened red rimmed eyes and gave him a look that pleaded for the answer she needed to hear. "I'm so sorry, honey. The paramedics didn't see Bear at the house, but I'm sure he's fine. He may be old, but he's a smart fellow. He'll be waiting someplace safe. You'll see." Tom squeezed her hand as a new flood of silent tears made fresh tracks down her face.

"But I promised him, Tom. I promised him! If something happens to him, I won't have kept my promise." Tom looked at her, his brows creased with worry. All this confused rambling was making him very concerned.

"Who?" Tom asked confused. "What did you promise? Who did you make a promise to?"

"Bear," Lisa replied simply. "I promised Bear he would see green grass once more. We were watching the robins bobbing around in the snow, and I told him we just had to have faith like the robins do, that spring will come. I promised him he would see another spring." Lisa started to cry in earnest now.

"I know he's getting old. I know he won't be with us much longer, but I just couldn't stand the thought of losing him in the winter. I know it doesn't make any sense, but winter is so hard on him. I wanted him to have some happy, easy days once more before his time comes."

Tears were welling up in Tom's eyes now, and he fought for control. "He's going to be okay, honey. I'm going to go home and find him, and he'll be waiting for you when you come home. You'll see. Now why don't you get some rest while I'm gone and I'll be back as soon as I have everything settled at home, okay?"

Lisa nodded and swiped at her wet cheeks. "Just go find him, please. Please find him."

Tom grabbed his jacket and headed out into the storm. It was going to be a slow drive to the house with the roads as icy as they were. He was going to have to put his worry aside and concentrate on his driving.

He'd be no help to Bear or Lisa if he ended up stranded in a ditch somewhere!

Chapter Three

Bear plodded on ahead, moving slower now. His coat was completely iced over, and he was beginning to shiver uncontrollably. He had to find someplace to get warm. He knew now, that he had become separated from Lisa. He also knew he wasn't near home any more. The path he was on was more rugged now, but he could tell it was a trail that had been travelled fairly recently. He stepped gingerly along its icy route, head down, trying to keep the cold, stabbing pellets out of his eyes. As he moved along, the tree cover became thicker and provided some protection from the weather. His old arthritic legs were tiring rapidly. He had to find shelter and stop for a while. Then he would resume his search for home. He had an overwhelming feeling that Lisa needed him, and he knew he would find his way back to her no matter what it took.

Suddenly Bear felt the force of the icy rain diminish. He sensed closeness in his surroundings that suggested maybe he was in a thicket, or maybe under an outcropping of rock. His instincts warned him to stay put and not venture any further into his new found haven. Going any further might mean getting tangled in thorny under brush, or falling into an unexpected ravine. He felt sturdy ground under his feet right here, and enough protection from the elements to provide warmth for rest. He would lie down right here and gather back some of his strength. Then he would continue his quest for home.

Tom made it home in far less time that he expected. The salt trucks had been out all day in anticipation of the storm, and the roads were almost decent. The most treacherous part of his journey had been navigating the long winding driveway at the house. Their contacted snow removal guy hadn't yet made it to their property to sand, and the drive was basically a skating rink. Taking it slow and easy, he had arrived at the foot of the drive and parked in front of the house. He looked hopefully towards the front verandah hoping that a big black form would be curled up by the door. His hopes were dashed, when he realized the porch was empty and there was no big black dog anywhere in sight. Stepping carefully out onto the ice, he made his way to the porch, using first the car, and then the branches of the bushes that lined the walkway for support. When he finally made it onto the porch, he started calling aloud for Bear. The big covered verandah wrapped around the entire house and Tom went from side to side calling and watching for any signs of movement. His heart sank as no sign of Bear appeared.

Heading inside, Tom couldn't help but hope that maybe someone had found Bear, and let him in. He opened the door, holding his breath and hoping against hope that this might be true. The silence and emptiness that greeted him was all the answer he needed. Bear was not in here, and was not anywhere nearby outside.

Tom sank into the big overstuffed armchair near the window. Today the view out across the property did not bring him the sense of serenity and beauty that it usually did. Today, the landscape looked bleak and threatening.

"Where are you Bear?" he spoke aloud. "Please be safe. I'm coming to find you." Tom headed into the bedroom to change into appropriate outdoor clothes. He dressed first in jeans and an old sweatshirt, and then donned water proof pants and jacket. He stepped into his winter hikers and pulled on warm gloves and a hat. He wasn't at all sure where to begin. Their property was large, and there was no way he could know which direction Bear had taken. He assumed that Bear would have headed along the drive where he and Lisa generally walked in the winter. From there, Tom would have to assume that he ended up out on the main road, or, if he veered off the driveway, then he would have ended up in the woods to the east of the property. Tom's mind raced as he imagined all the possible fates that could have befallen their old friend. He could have made it onto the road and been hit by a car. Maybe he was at the animal hospital, or maybe an uncaring driver hit him and didn't stop. Maybe he was lying out here in a ditch, cold and injured. Maybe he just got so tired he laid down, fell asleep and never woke up. Tom shook his head. He had to be more positive. Bear was a survivor. He would want to get back to Lisa. Tom tried to think of happier scenarios as he plodded along the icy road. If Bear had made it to the main road, then maybe he had made it to help. Their closest neighbor was just a mile down the road. He could have seen Bear and taken him in. "Why didn't I check the answering machine?" Tom admonished himself. "There might have been word on there of Bear's whereabouts." Tom debated whether to turn around and go check, or keep on searching. He was out here now, so he would give it a little more time. If he didn't find anything soon, he would head home. Thoughts of having to return to Lisa without some form of reassurance added to his already mounting worry.

The blowing snow and subsequent freezing rain didn't leave Tom any tracks that he could follow. The snow wasn't deep enough or consistently deep enough for Bear to have made a trail through it. There were patches of clear ground, patches of slushy areas and patches of deeper snow scattered throughout the property due to the changing weather patterns of spring. There were no telltale signs of a dog, or any animal for that matter having gone through here. Tom had to assume that Bear had continued on down the main road, or had headed in a different direction altogether. He honestly didn't have any clue how they would ever find him. Their property backed onto acres and acres of conservation woodlands. If Bear was somewhere in the woods, the odds of finding him alive and well were slim to none. Tom heaved a heavy sigh and turned around, planning out his next moves as he battled the freezing drizzle that stung his face. He decided to go home and check the answering machine. If there was nothing there, he would change his clothes again, grab a bite to eat and stop at his neighbor, Jim Barrow's place just in case Bear had made it that far. Then he would head back to the hospital, hopefully with some positive news for Lisa. She really didn't need this kind of stress right now. The doctors had warned him of the importance of keeping her quiet and calm to let the pregnancy get back on track. This baby had already had a rocky start and this latest scare could very well get Lisa all worked up again. They had almost lost the baby early in the pregnancy when Lisa had contracted a severe case of bacterial pneumonia. Since then she had been super diligent about the foods she ate, the amount of exercise she undertook, and the stress she handled in her job. They were "older" first time parents as it was, having not been able to get pregnant as quickly as they had hoped. Now, at 35 Lisa was already considered to be at higher risk for complications. All of these thoughts ran together through Tom's head as he trudged back through the snow and ice.

Once home, he quickly removed his outerwear and headed to the kitchen to check for messages. His heart sank when he saw from across the room that the red light indicating there was a message was off. He went to the phone and picked up the handset just to be sure. There was nothing. In a last ditch attempt for some good news, he checked for messages on his cell phone too. Nothing there either. His last hope was that Bear had made it to the neighbors, or they had seen him on the road and picked him up. Maybe they hadn't been able to call because of the weather. He would know the outcome of that hope soon enough. His gut was telling him it was a long shot, but his heart held on to the hope.

Once he had changed to dry clothes, he pulled on his regular winter jacket and headed back to the car. Jim Barrow was a retired school principal, so he should be home. He didn't like to venture out in any kind of weather, so Tom was certain he'd be there. Sure enough, his knock was answered almost immediately by the tall, distinguished looking older man. Jim smiled and greeted Tom warmly.

"Hello neighbor! What brings you here on such a blustery day?"

"Hi, Jim," Tom responded. "Glad to see you're keeping warm and dry. I was hoping that maybe you had seen my dog. Do you remember Bear? He seems to have wandered off."

"Of course, I remember him," Jim nodded. "That old rascal is not a dog you'd soon forget! As I recall, he was rather fond of the ducks in my pond when you folks would walk by! I'd know him for sure, but I haven't seen him lately."

Tom's shoulders drooped and his hands fell to his sides. "Well, there goes my last ray of hope. I thought maybe he wandered down the road a piece and found his way here, or that you had seen him on the road and took him in."

Jim shook his head. "Nope, neither one. I sure wasn't driving anywhere in this storm, and I haven't seen him around the house. Sorry, neighbor."

"Well thanks anyway," Tom shook the older man's hand. "I'd really appreciate it if you kept an eye out for him. "

"Of course," Jim replied. "I'll let you know right away if I see any signs of him. Good luck!" Tom thanked him and headed back out into the weather. The freezing rain had finally stopped and the wind now held just a bit of warmth. Spring really wasn't that far off. They just needed to find Bear and then they could look forward to it.

Chapter Four

Bear opened his eyes and raised his big head. Every bone in his body ached. But he could tell that the storm had passed and his ever keen sense of smell picked up the trace of warmth that was now on the wind. But he could feel another sense of warmth too, and another unfamiliar scent. He turned his head in the direction of the smell and came nose to nose with another body. Tucked up against his flank a scrawny snoring puppy slept with his nose buried in Bear's long fur. Bear nudged the tiny body into wakefulness and the pup immediately started licking Bear's jowls. Suddenly Bear forgot his aches and pains, and even the fact that he was lost. Here was another creature that needed his help. He reached out a big paw and brought the little pup in closer, licking fur that was matted and covered with grunge. Bear thought he even tasted a bit of blood matted on the fur as well. All of his nurturing instincts kicked into gear and Bear soon had the pup clean and warm. The two dogs remained tucked into the root outcropping for another few hours, and then Bear decided it was time to start looking for home again. Now that he was warmer, and rested, he was suddenly aware of his gnawing hunger and thirst. He was sure the pup was in need of food as well, and Bear knew it was time to get moving.

The sun was shining now, and the snow that the storm had brought was melting quickly. It would be easier travelling now. Bear nudged the pup into motion and headed back along the trail he had taken the day before. With the snow melting, the well-worn trail was much easier to find and Bear was filled with a renewed sense of hope.

This was his trail, the trail that he had walked almost every day of his life with Lisa. If he followed this trail, he was certain he would find home.

Bear and the pup set off. Although Bear couldn't see him, he was aware that the pup kept wandering off to investigate whatever caught his attention along the way. A single woof from Bear brought him back into line and they continued on. They found a portion of the stream that was beginning to thaw and stopped for a long, much needed drink. Then off they went again in search of home.

After a while the two weary travelers stopped in a clearing under some tall pines for a rest. The ground was covered with a blanket of fallen pine needles, and although it was damp, it was soft on Bears old achy bones. Bear settled in for a rest, hoping that the pup would do the same. It wasn't long before Bear fell into a deep sleep. Instead of doing the same, the curious pup decided to investigate a nearby thicket, where he was certain he could smell rabbits. Deeper into the twisted vines he crawled, skirting through the bushes on his belly. Bear slept soundly, as only old dogs can do, unaware of the dangers that his adventurous travelling companion had wandered into. Opening his eyes some time later and sensing that the pup was gone, Bear gave a single woof to guide him back. Bear stood still, waiting for the pup to push up against him, licking his face and trying to get approval for what he had done. Bear waited and barked again. Oh how he wished he could hear! Still he felt no nearby movement. Raising his nose into the wind, Bear determined which direction the pup had gone and headed out. His old deaf ears were unable to hear the whimpering of the frightened pup whose leg had become entangled in a web of twisted, thorny branches. Once snarled, the more the pup moved, the more the branches twisted around his leg. He was gnawing frantically at them when Bear finally reached him. Bear tread carefully towards the pup's movement, trying to avoid getting himself caught in the thorns. He nuzzled the terrified pup to calm him down, and then crawled as close to the pup as he could, using his nose to figure out what needed to be done. Bear was able to work away at the branches with some care as long as the pup remained still. He was deep into his task when his nose suddenly caught a different scent on the wind. He abandoned the tangles and held his head high drinking in every bit of the new scent that he could. They had been found!

Chapter Five

Tom was growing weary and discouraged. He had trudged for a good hour searching the west side of the property, all to no avail. He had then circled around and started in the opposite direction, knowing that Bear could be anywhere. He might even be just a few yards away from him, hidden by the dense trees and scrub of the woods. There was no use in calling out, or hoping that Bear would hear him, and that just made the search more frustrating. The underbrush was getting thicker now, and several times Tom had to disentangle his feet from the thorny branches. He had already fallen once when his foot got caught in a web of tangled vines. It was getting almost impossible to venture any further into the woods. Tom stood for a minute, getting his bearings and trying to decide what to do next.

It was in that quiet moment that he heard a sound. It was faint, and a ways off to his left, but it definitely sounded like a dog whimpering. Tom listened for another few seconds, and then followed the sounds. Stepping as carefully as he could, he walked and kept his ears focused on the sounds that were slowly coming closer. Instinct trumped logic and he started calling Bear's name, no longer thinking about Bear not being able to hear him.

"Bear! Bear! Where are you big fella? Bear!" Tom shouted over and over, pausing in between to be sure he was still heading in the right direction. He suddenly realized that the more he yelled, the more frequent the whimpering became. His heart started to pound with fear. The whimpering sounds could only mean that Bear was hurt. They were not the sort of sounds that a big dog like Bear would normally make. Tom picked up the pace and was relieved to find himself in a bit of a clearing. Now he could hear the sounds of breaking twigs along with the whimpering. He hurried across the clearing to the edge of the woods, where he could now see movement. Pushing aside another gnarl of branches, Tom found himself looking right into Bear's big brown eyes. The old dog was waiting for him, tail wagging and body quivering with happiness.

As Tom approached, he noticed the smaller dog entangled in the vines, and realized that he was the source of the sounds that had led him to their location. He spoke softly to the pup as he approached.

"Okay, boy. Just take it easy. I'm going to get you out of this thicket. Just stay still, ok?" Tom worked quickly to get the little pup free. He could see matted fur where blood from previous cuts was beginning to dry, and new cuts from this latest ordeal were starting to bleed. The pup was shivering and obviously suffering from exposure as well. Tom knew he had to work fast if he was going to save the little guy. Bear stood off to the side, patiently waiting for his master to finish.

With the pup was finally free and tucked inside Tom's coat, the tired but happy trio headed for home. Somehow, the way home seemed a lot shorter and soon they were all inside enjoying the warmth. Tom filled a water bowl right away and both dogs drank till the bowl was dry. He gave Bear a good rubdown with one of Lisa's fluffiest towels, knowing that she would not object. Bear languished in the wonderful feel of Tom's hands massaging his old tired bones, and then stretched himself out on the thick braided rug in front of the fireplace. Tom got the fire roaring and got Bear settled before turning his attentions to the pup. He settled the pup beside Bear on the rug while he gathered some supplies. He filled a big pot with warm water and grabbed a few of the older towels from the bathroom along with antiseptic spray and some gauze pads. Little by little, he dabbed and patted each bloodied area on the pup's coat, applying antiseptic cleanser as he went and then drying him off with fresh clean towels. Eventually the pup started to look somewhat normal and Tom was surprised to see how much white there actually was in his coat. The black and white markings suggested to Tom that he was probably part Border collie although there was also another prominent breed in there as well. All in all, he was quite a cute little thing, and a lot fuzzier than he had at first appeared.

"Lisa is going to love you," Tom thought as he continued to dry the pup's coat. The more he worked, the fuzzier his fur became, confirming Tom's initial thoughts that the pup was not very old. He was also very thin, making Tom think that he had probably been separated from his mother long before being properly weaned. Food was definitely the next thing on the agenda for both dogs, but given the pups young age, Tom knew that Bear's food would not be suitable. Instead, he prepared a bowl of oatmeal topped with a bit of cream, and then gave each dog his food. Bear ate hungrily and the pup devoured the oatmeal without hesitation. Now warm, fed and dry, the two dogs curled up by the fire for some much needed rest.

Tom couldn't wait to get back to the hospital to share the good news with Lisa. Knowing that Bear was safe and sound at home would finally help her relax. He wasn't really sure what they would do about the puppy, but there was time enough to deal with that later. Right now he just wanted to see her and tell her the news. Tom went through the house quickly and shut the doors to all the adjoining rooms, and removed anything that looked like it might be dangerous for an inquisitive puppy from the living room. Then, satisfied that Bear would keep a watchful eye on the newcomer, Tom headed back to the hospital.

Chapter Six

Lisa was smiling from ear to ear. "I can't believe you found him! I was so sure that he was lost forever! Now I just want to get home and hug his scruffy old neck!" Tom laughed.

"It's good to see that beautiful smile of yours again. And I know Bear is waiting for that hug! But there is something else you need to know." Lisa looked at Tom and a look of worry began to creep back into her eyes. Tom was quick to reassure her.

"No, no. It's nothing bad.....nothing to worry about. It's just that Bear wasn't alone when I found him." Tom explained about the pup and filled her in on his present condition. "He seems to be fine, but I think I should run him into Dr. McKay just to be sure."

"Maybe he'll have some idea who he belongs to," Lisa added, "although finding a young pup lost and alone in the woods sounds a lot like abandonment to me. In which case no one will ever know where he came from."

"That is very likely," Tom agreed. "At any rate, we can have him checked out, make sure he's healthy and then either try to find a home for him or turn him over to one of the local rescue organizations." Lisa nodded. The option of them keeping a puppy was not on the table. For a time Lisa had considered getting a puppy while Bear was still with them to help lessen the loneliness when he was gone. But they had discussed it at length and had finally decided that it would not be fair to bring a new puppy into Bear's life at this point. As much as they both loved dogs, they couldn't do that to their beloved and loyal friend. Lisa had often wished that they had adopted two dogs when they got Bear, or had taken in another dog when he was still young, but to do it now, in what were his final days with them just seemed wrong.

"Those are both good options," Lisa said in response to Tom's suggestions. "But let's get me home and him to Dr. McKay before we do anything else." Tom smiled and gave her a big hug.

"Absolutely. Now let's find out what we have to do to get you out of here!" Within the hour the doctor had signed the discharge papers and they had packed up Lisa's things. Wheeling her down to the lobby in the wheel chair, they joked about Lisa enjoying this pampering she was getting now, because very soon she would be busy with all the challenges of being a new Mom.

Lisa couldn't believe how good it felt to be home. She had only been in the hospital for two days yet it had seemed like forever. Bear struggled to his feet at the sight of her and Lisa embraced him before she even took off her coat. Bear wagged his entire back end in happiness, and their new furry houseguest joined in the ruckus, jumping in circles around Bear and trying to kiss Lisa's face. Lisa laughed with pure joy, as Tom looked on, thinking that her laughter was the most beautiful sound he had ever heard. The pup soon drowned out all other sounds, however, when his excitement erupted into a high pitched puppy bark. Bear growled a warning that he had better behave, and Tom and Lisa laughed.

"You tell him, Bear." Tom joked. "You show him whose boss."

Eventually things calmed down and once the dogs had been let out to tend to their business, they were once again ready to settle. Tom brought Lisa a hot cup of herbal tea and announced that he was going to run the pup over to the vet, asking Lisa to promise that she would rest while he was gone.

"Could you wait just a bit?" she asked. "He appears to be fine, and I would like to come along when you take him. I want to hear what Dr. McKay has to say, and also ask him what he recommends we do with him."

Tom hesitated for a moment, not sure whether or not it was a good idea for her to be up and about so soon. Lisa knew exactly what he was thinking.

"I'm fine," she said in the definite tone that told Tom her mind was already made up. "A little jaunt into town isn't going to harm anything." Tom relented, and sat while she finished her tea.

Chapter Seven

The trip into town was noisy and left little opportunity for conversation. It was obvious the little pup had never travelled in a moving vehicle before and he was very vocal about his fear. He yelped and howled constantly even though Lisa held him in her arms for the entire trip. Bear was blissfully unaware of the commotion and was content to sprawl himself across the back seat and snore his way through the journey. By the time they reached Dr. McKay's office, Lisa and Tom were nearly at their wits end. Tom practically jumped out of the car and hurried to open Lisa's door and release the pup from the confines of the car. He wasn't any happier about being on a leash, however, so their struggles were not yet over. As Tom dragged the pup towards the clinic door, Lisa gave Bear a comforting scratch and a cookie and told him that they would be right back. Bear managed to raise his head and chomp down the cookie before falling back into his doggy dreams. The pup pulled and tugged on the leash while Tom dragged him forward inch by inch. Deciding in the end, that he would need another tactic if they were ever going to actually make it up the steps and into the office, Tom finally hoisted the noisy fur ball into his arms and carried him, leaving the leash dangling in the mud as they went.

Dr. McKay was just coming out of one of the examining rooms as Lisa and Tom came through the door.

"Well, good afternoon, friends," he said cheerfully. "And who is this little fella?" As Tom explained, Dr. McKay led them back into the room he had just come from.

"Let's get him up here on the table and I'll have a look."

"He's a feisty little guy," Tom warned the doctor. "I don't think he's had any exposure to people and places outside of where he was born."

Dr. McKay smiled and concentrated on calming the pup so he could give him a thorough once over. A puzzled look crossed the old man's weathered face as he studied the pup.

"What is it Doc?" Tom inquired. "Something more serious than we thought?"

"No, no, not at all," the old doctor said shaking his head. "It's just that his markings are so similar to two other abandoned pups that have come in this past week. I'm starting to believe that they are all from the same litter."

A look of horror clouded Lisa eyes. "That was my first thought exactly. I was just so hoping it wouldn't be true. How could someone have just abandoned a new litter of pups? Just dump them off on the side of the road or off in the woods to fend for themselves?"

"As much as I hate to admit it, Lisa, things like that do happen. Sometimes folks just don't know what else to do. Sometimes they can't afford to feed the pups, or maybe they just don't want them and they don't want anybody to know. Sometimes they won't bring them into the shelter for fear they'll be judged or maybe charged a fee. There could be any number of reasons."

"None of which are acceptable," Lisa declared.

"I totally agree with you. But desperate people can sometimes do desperate things. And as much as I hate to say it, some people can be just plain heartless. Anyway, this little guy looks to be in pretty good shape overall. He's just a bit dehydrated. I'd like to keep him here overnight with an IV in to replenish his fluids. Then you can come get your new puppy back tomorrow."

Tom spoke up quickly. "Well, we don't have any plans to keep him. We just wanted to get him some help. I guess he'll have to be turned over to the shelter as soon as he's well." Tom didn't like the look that was settling on Lisa's face. He knew she was torn. Her heart and her head were obviously fighting over what she should do.

She would feel guilty no matter what. Guilty for not keeping the pup and guilty for forcing a new pup on Bear. It was a no win situation. She looked at Tom for help and he couldn't think of a word to say. It was a good thing the vet wanted to keep the pup overnight. At least that would give them some time to talk and mull things over.

"If you want, just give me a call tomorrow and I can call the authorities to come get him, the kind vet offered."

"No, we'll come back either way," Tom assured the vet. "If we decide not to keep him, then we'll take him to the shelter ourselves."

"It's up to you," Dr. McKay said as he shook Tom's hand. "I do appreciate you doing that, though. It'd be one less thing on my plate. I'm kinda shorthanded here this week. The storm knocked the power out at my assistant Carol's house and she has taken a few days off to handle damage control."

"It's our pleasure," Tom said as they left. "See you tomorrow then, and thanks Doc."

This time the ride home was quiet. Lisa was deep in thought and kept glancing into the back seat at Bear. Bear was her dog, and Tom didn't feel right offering an opinion unless she asked him. Keeping the pup or giving it up was going to have to be her decision. Finally, she turned to Tom with an anguished expression. "I feel horrible thinking of that little pup going to a shelter and maybe being put down because no one wants him. But I look at Bear and I think he deserves to live out his last days in peace and quiet and with a routine that he's familiar with. You can't bring a puppy home and not expect it to bring chaos into the picture. I just don't think I can do that to Bear."

Tom's heart went out to her and he reached across the seat to squeeze her hand. "It's ok, honey," he said gently. "You're perfectly justified in putting Bear's needs first. He has been by your side for a long time and deserves your complete devotion. But I think you should probably be more optimistic where the pup is concerned. Nowadays, most rescue dogs go to foster homes until they are adopted. He doesn't necessarily have to go to a shelter where they might not be able to keep him. We can check around and see what rescue groups operate around here. A good healthy pup like him is sure to be adopted without any trouble. So stop worrying and start relaxing. You have another person who needs you too you know." Lisa smiled and squeezed his hand.

"You're absolutely right. Let's go home!"

Chapter Eight

After an easy relaxed morning, Lisa was starting to feel like her old self again. All in all her pregnancy had been pretty normal, and it was good to know that things should proceed that way now for the next couple of months. The weather, too had improved and she could almost start to believe that the latest storm was the last. The temperature had risen steadily to melt the remaining snow, and once again the brave little crocuses poked new buds up to the sun. Bear seemed to move about a lot easier with the coming of warmer weather. She supposed dogs were a lot like people in that the cold often made old ailments flare up. It still tugged at her heart to see him aging, and she tried hard to give him extra love and care at every opportunity. It lifted her spirits to know that he would enjoy this coming spring. A chubby robin bounced across the lawn as she stood deep in her thoughts, and without thinking, she put her fingers to her lips, brought them down to her hand, and then stamped her hand with her opposite fist, just as she had always done as a child. Back then she truly believed that stamping robins in the spring brought good luck, and today she wanted to believe it too. If wishing could make it so, then Bear would indeed enjoy another spring.

By early afternoon they were ready to head back over to the clinic to pick up the pup. Unless something had changed since yesterday, their plan was to bring him home for just a day or two until they found the right rescue group to take him. Lisa hoped that Bear would understand. Tom had already looked up the numbers of three groups, and the animal care worker that gave them to him had seemed very positive that one of them would have a foster home available.

"Tom, Lisa," Dr. McKay greeted them as they walked in. "I'm happy to say that your new little friend is doing just fine and will be able to leave with you today. But something new developed this morning that I thought you might be interested in knowing."

Lisa and Tom looked at him, waiting for him to continue. "One of the drivers from the bakery that delivers to the local grocers brought in a sick dog he found in the parking lot. She's in pretty bad shape I'm afraid, but after a close examination and considering the pups that have been brought in the past couple of days, I'm willing to bet that this poor little lady is the mother to all three of those pups. My guess is she got sick and the pups ran off looking for food and shelter. I think Mama has about done herself in trying to find them and care for them."

"Oh, the poor thing," Lisa gasped. Her eyes filled with tears. "Can I see her? I'd like to give her some comfort." Dr. McKay led them into the examining room where a shaggy black and white dog was lying still on the table. She was a medium sized dog, obviously with a lot of collie in her. Her coat was matted and damp over her thin frame and the eyes that looked back at Lisa were glazed over and distant.

"I've given her something to make her comfortable," Dr. McKay said. Lisa approached the table and knelt at the dog's head. In a soft voice, she soothed the dog and ran her fingers through the matted fur.

"It's okay, girl," Lisa crooned. "Your pups are in good hands now, and you can rest." As Lisa continued to speak, the dog looked up at her. Suddenly a sense of familiarity came over Lisa as she looked back into the sorrowful eyes. "Look! She has one blue eye and one brown. I think I know this dog," she said suddenly, as recognition dawned. "I've seen her before. She belongs to a woman who comes into the local food bank, where I volunteer. She always brought the dog with her, and was always asking if anyone had donated dog food."

"Do you know the woman's name, or where she lives?" Tom asked. Lisa thought for a moment.

"No, I don't think she ever said. But maybe the folks at the food bank would know. Maybe the dog ran off and she's looking for her. I think we should go talk to them."

"I agree," said Tom. "Doc would you mind if the pup stays here just a bit longer? We'll be back before you close up for the night."

"No problem," Doc replied. "Take your time. I'd like to find out who this pretty lady belongs to."

Lisa gave the dog a final pat and then turned to leave with Tom. "Take care of her Doctor. Hopefully we can come back with some good news!"

Tom started the car and cast a concerned look towards Lisa. "Are you sure you want to take all this on? You just got out of the hospital, and the Doctor said to take things easy." Lisa shook her head and shrugged.

"I just keep thinking about how I felt when Bear was lost. What if that poor old woman is searching for her dog too? And if I remember correctly, she wasn't a picture of health the last time I saw her. I really want to find her and put her mind at ease." Tom recognized the determined note in Lisa's voice and simply nodded.

"Let's just hope, then, that the folks at the food bank have some information. Otherwise I don't know how we would ever track her down." Lisa was silent for the remainder of the trip turning only every so often to cast a loving look towards Bear who snored away in the back seat, completely oblivious to all the worry of his master.

Chapter Nine

The food bank looked especially busy as Tom and Lisa drove up. They had arrived a good fifteen minutes before it was due to open and already there was a long line of tired and cold looking folks waiting to get inside. Just the sight of them tugged at Lisa's heart and made her eyes fill with tears. "Being pregnant sure makes a person emotional," she thought to herself. "But we are so blessed," she whispered more to herself than to anyone else, as she scanned the line of people. She was hoping that the old woman might be among the crowd, but Lisa didn't think any of the women in line looked familiar.

By the time they had parked the car and walked across the parking lot, the line had started to move inside. Taking pity on those waiting outside in the cold, the woman in charge had opened the doors a bit early. Tom and Lisa fell in behind the last few people heading in, and then headed directly to the supervisor's office at the back of the large shelf lined room.

An elderly woman with thick glasses and a full head of curly white hair greeted them pleasantly. She listened closely as Lisa explained about the lost dog and abandoned puppies, and about the lady that Lisa believed was a frequent visitor to the food bank.

"I don't really remember what the lady looked like, except that she was elderly and seemed rather frail. But I do remember seeing the dog and remarking on her unusual eyes. I also remember her saying that she hoped there would be some dog food donations."

The friendly smile that had previously brightened the supervisors face now held a look of concern and compassion. "I do believe I know the woman you're referring to. We do have several regulars that come in looking for dog food, but I remember her because she did seem so frail. I was always worried that she was concentrating more on feeding her dog than herself."

"Do you remember her name?" Tom asked hopefully.

"No," the woman replied slowly, rubbing her thumb across her chin. "But I think she may have left contact information in our registration book. She said she had some difficulty arranging transportation in so she couldn't always check in on a regular basis.

She wanted us to call her when we had dog food donations come in. Let me see if I can find it." The woman walked briskly for someone her age, and with a sense of purpose. She was obviously a person who wasted no time when it came to getting a job done. She thumbed through a binder on her desk, and suddenly slapped her hand down on the page. "Here it is," she declared triumphantly. "Name, address and phone number. I'm pretty sure that this is who we're looking for."

She rummaged through her desk drawer and found a pad of paper, quickly jotting the information down and then tearing the sheet of for Lisa. "I hope you find her."

"Me too," Lisa replied, beaming. "Thank you so much. I'll let you know what happens." Grabbing Tom's arm she pulled him out of the office and past the clump of people filling their baskets with much needed food items. Tom was grateful to be leaving. He too, felt deeply for those who were less fortunate than himself and it was all he could do to not stay behind and offer a friendly ear for conversation or a genuine offer of help in any way. He made a mental note to pin his card to the bulletin board inside offering free handyman help for anyone who might need it.

Lisa was excited to get moving. "It says here she lives at 6657 Durwood Lane. That's about eight miles out of town. We should be able to be there in about ten minutes right?" she asked looking at Tom.

"About that," Tom replied. "Some of the roads out that way are pretty winding, but it definitely won't take us long." As they headed along the narrow country road, Lisa couldn't help but wonder why someone like Millie Driscoll lived way out here in such a remote area. Lisa hoped she had family or at the very least good neighbors who kept an eye on her.

Almost within ten minutes exactly, they were pulling into a long gravel laneway. Snow remained along the shaded edges of the lane that was bordered by tall scraggly looking pine trees. Very little sunlight got in here to melt it away, and Lisa silently wondered if the snow would stay right through until summer.

Tom's voice broke through her thoughts. "Mighty isolated location for an old woman on her own," he said.

"Well, we don't know for sure that she is on her own, but it did sound like it." The driveway came to an abrupt halt in front of a small weathered cabin. There were places where you could tell it had once been painted a bright sunny yellow but now it was nearly all a dreary shade of gray. The windows were dingy and the front steps looked treacherous.

Tom and Lisa got out of the car and stood for a moment unsure just what to do now that they had come this far. Tom spoke first. "I feel kind of strange just arriving like this out of the blue," he said. "Maybe we should have called first." Lisa shrugged.

"We probably should have, but we're here now, so we might as well see what's up. I just hope we don't scare her out of her skin!"

"Be careful on these steps," Tom cautioned, taking Lisa firmly by the arm. Once safely established on the porch, they knocked hesitantly at the door. When no response came, Tom knocked a little louder. Still no answer came from within. Lisa tried to peer through the window of the door, but a heavy fabric curtain blocked her view.

"Maybe she's not home," Tom said when another substantial knock went unanswered. Lisa was shaking her head.

"I think she's in there, Tom. I'm just getting a really bad feeling that something's wrong." Lisa now stepped up to the door and knocked even louder. When there was still no response, Tom picked his way back down the broken stairs and fought through a tangle of overgrown garden to get to the side of the cabin. Standing on tip toe, he could see into the room from a small window. The curtains in this room had been pulled back and he could see the outlines of furniture and appliances. Across the small open space he could see an old worn sofa and chair. There were no lights on inside, but he was sure he could see someone lying on the couch. The form was still and covered with blankets.

"I think I could see someone lying on the couch," he said to Lisa as he clambered back up the steps. "Do you think we should go in? She might be in trouble." Lisa nodded as she stepped forward and took the grimy old door knob in her hand. It was loose and felt like it was going to come off in her hand if she tried to turn it. Holding it securely, she tuned the knob and gave the weathered cedar door a gentle push. It creaked open easily, and Lisa called out as opened it further.

"Hello? Hello? Is there anybody here? Mrs. Driscoll? Are you here?" Lisa stopped for a minute to let her eyes adjust to the gloomy inside. A muffled sound came from the direction of the living room. "Mrs. Driscoll?" Lisa called softly as she approached the the moaning form under the blankets. Bending closer to the now quiet form, Lisa spoke again. "Mrs. Driscoll? I'm Lisa Portland, and this is my husband Tom. We got your name and address form the folks at the food bank. We wanted to ask you about your dog." At the sound of the word dog, the old lady started mumbling.

"Sadie. Sadie."

"Okay, okay," Lisa tried to calm her. "Let's get you a drink of water and then we'll talk." Lisa motioned towards the kitchen area. Tom quickly found a glass and filled it with cool water from the tap. Surprisingly enough, given the state of disrepair everywhere else, the tiny kitchen was spotless and organized. While Tom got the water, Lisa plumped the pillows up behind the woman so she could have a drink. Lisa put the glass gently to her lips, and the woman took a small sip before collapsing back against the pillows. A wrinkled hand with gnarled knuckles reached out to take Lisa's arm.

"Have you found my Sadie?" the weak voice implored.

"I think we may have," Lisa said slowly. "Did Sadie run away?" The old woman took a deep breath and then let out a ragged sigh.

"Sadie was going to have puppies. I made her a bed and everything over there so she could have them inside out of the weather. A bony finger pointed to the far corner of the living room. It was almost her time and then I got sick. I remember putting Sadie in the box and telling her to be strong. Then I went to lie down here. I was having a terrible pain in my head and couldn't stay awake. When I woke up again, Sadie was gone. I guess the inside door was ajar and she must have let herself out. I couldn't get up to find her. I don't know if she had her pups or not. I just don't remember any of it." At this point the old woman started to cry.

"It's okay, now" Lisa assured her. "We're here and we're going to help you. You just rest. My husband and I are just going to chat for a minute. You just rest." Lisa turned to Tom, nodding for him to follow her. Once they were out of earshot, Lisa spoke. "She must have been out for a few days! What do we do now?" she asked Tom, obviously flustered by what had just happened.

"The first thing we should do is call 911 and get an ambulance out here. Let's get her into the hospital where the doctors can find out what's wrong. When she's stronger, we can talk with her some more."

"You're right," Lisa agreed. Tom was already punching the numbers into his cell phone.

Chapter Ten

Millie Driscoll had never been in a hospital before. Well at least not as a patient. She had been so healthy all of her 74 years and the longest time she had spent in a hospital was when her husband George was sick. He had passed away within these very walls and Millie had sworn when she left after that, that she would never come back. Now here she was, lying in one of the sterile white rooms covered with starchy, scratchy sheets and listening to the blips and bleeps of an array of gray machines.

In the distance, she could hear muffled voices and now and then a few chortles as nurses and doctors sought to add brightness to their otherwise somber surroundings. Millie looked round the room with much confusion. She forced her brain to try and recall how she had ended up here. It was a challenging task. The old gray matter just didn't work like it used to. Sometimes just remembering what she had done ten minutes ago was an effort in itself. But this time, she could feel her heart working hard to provide the details of her situation. Sadie. All she had to do was think about her beloved Sadie and it all came flooding back. A growing fear that she might never see her dog again brought fresh tears to her eyes. And then there was that young couple who had arrived at the house to help her. Millie struggled to recall the names. Tim....no, Tom. Tom and Lisa. And then, as though she had projected her thoughts into reality, a soft voice spoke beside her.

"Hello, Millie. I'm Lisa. Do you remember me?"

Millie smiled, thin lips stretching into a grin bordered by wrinkles. "I do remember you dear. Thank you so much for helping me. As much as I hate being in this place, I have to admit, I'm feeling a lot better for being here."

"I'm so glad," Lisa said squeezing her hand. "The doctor says there's nothing seriously wrong, and that you should be able to go home in a day or two."

"Oh, I was pretty sure there wasn't anything wrong with me. I haven't been eating all that well lately. I probably just got run down. Now tell me about my dog. You said at the house that you needed to talk to me about Sadie."

Lisa looked down at their clasped hands trying to figure out how to tell the old woman what she knew. As always, Lisa decided honesty was the best policy. In as succinct a manner as possible she explained about finding Bear and the puppy together and how the vet had figured out that there must have been a litter of pups all wandering around in the same vicinity. Lisa then explained about Sadie showing up at the animal clinic and told her how the vet had put two and two together.

Millie listened intently and let Lisa finish before she spoke. "So Sadie is at the vets along with one of the pups. The other two pups were taken in by the people who found them. Is that right?" Lisa nodded and was about to speak but Millie began talking again. "And all the pups were healthy? And is Sadie okay? She didn't suffer any ill effects from the whole ordeal?" Millie barely took a breath between questions.

"The vet said that all the pups were a little dehydrated and suffering from a bit of exposure, but nothing serious. He gave them all their first set of vaccinations and got them back to normal before he let them go." Then Lisa paused, breaking eye contact. Millie might have been elderly but she was still had a pretty sharp mind.

"What aren't you telling me?" she asked Lisa with concern.

Lisa hated to have to tell her the next part. "Sadie is still at the vets still, but she's in pretty bad shape. She apparently wandered around in that last storm for quite a while trying to find her pups. They had wandered off when their mom couldn't give them any milk."

"But is she going to be okay?" It broke Lisa's heart to hear the woman sound so hopeful.

She wanted so badly to give her some good news. Instead, she just shrugged.

"The vet says he'll do what he can. I can head on back there and then come give you a report if you like."

"Oh. Please do," Millie said grasping both of Lisa's hands in hers. "I would like someone to be with her, give her some comfort and love, until I can see her for myself."

Lisa gave her word that she would do just that, and promised to return with a report just as soon as she could. "In the meantime, you get some rest so you can get home." Millie gave a tired little nod and then sank back against the pale blue pillows, her small pale face almost disappearing into the folds of fabric.

Chapter Eleven

Lisa was tired. This whole ordeal was taking a pretty heavy toll on her, but she had to see it through to the end. There were so many little things that had to be figured out before she could put it all behind her and get on with just having this baby. Thank goodness none of this had had an adverse effect on her pregnancy. The baby had been her priority, and now that she was certain everything was okay in that department, she could concentrate on the rest of it.

 Bear was home and safe, and hadn't suffered any lasting ill effects from his outdoor adventure. The pup that they had found with Bear was also in pretty good shape. The vet had sutured a couple of deeper cuts, but all in all his injuries were minor. A good night's sleep in a warm bed and some good food had worked wonders. Her main concern now was for Sadie. When Lisa had left the vets to go find Millie, the poor dog had been pretty unresponsive. Lisa feared what she might face when she returned. All of these thoughts whirled around in her head while she waited for Tom to bring the car to the front doors of the hospital. He had waited with Bear while she visited Millie and now they were heading back to the Dr. McKay's office as promised.

Lisa fastened her seat back and let her head fall back against the headrest, sighing deeply. Tom cast a concerned look in her direction. "Are you okay?" he asked.

Lisa turned her head without lifting it. "I'm fine. Just tired and worried. It's going to be really hard on Millie if something happens to that dog." Tom reached across the seat and patted Lisa's knee.

"Given where and how she lives, I'm willing to bet that old lady is a lot stronger than you give her credit for. Oh, I'm sure she'll take it hard if something happens, but I have a hunch she'll be able to handle it." Lisa looked at him and tried to smile.

"You always think the best of people. That's one of the reasons I fell in love with you."

Tom chuckled. "Oh yeah? Want to share some of the other ones?"

"Not right now," Lisa joked back. "I'm way too tired to work my brain that hard!" They both laughed and the next time Tom looked over, she had drifted off into a sound sleep. He was almost sorry when they pulled up to the animal hospital a few minutes later. She just looked so peaceful. He reached over and shook her shoulder gently.

"Wake up sleeping beauty," he said. "We're here."

It was almost closing time for the clinic so the parking lot was empty except for Dr. McKay's car and one other minivan. The side doors of the van were open and Lisa could see children getting settled into their seats. A very excited puppy was adding to the chaos and interfering with their efforts to get situated. The pup was obviously being reunited with his kids after an absence and wanted to show his delight by licking each of their faces in turn. Lisa smiled, knowing full well how wonderful it felt to be reunited with a pet. As a child she had always hated having to leave their dogs at a kennel. And she related only too well to the wonders of being reunited, thinking in particular about Bear. She also tried to ignore the nagging little worry in her head as she said a silent prayer in her heart that the dog they were about to check on would also be reunited with her owner.

Dr. McKay came out of the back room wiping his hands on a towel, a deep frown creasing his brow. He looked up and tried to force a smile for Tom and Lisa. To their expectant looks, he just shook his head. Lisa felt the tears well up.

"I'm sorry," the vet said. "She's just too far gone. She must have hemorrhaged after delivering the pups. I suspect she passed out and that is why they wandered off. Then wandering around herself trying to find them was just more than her body could take. I've done all I can to make her comfortable, but she's barely breathing."

"I want to be with her." Lisa said, making her way past the doctor without invitation. "I promised Millie I'd be with her. I have to be with her. I have to tell her how much Millie loves her." Lisa was sobbing now, and as much as Tom wanted to stop her from going in there, he had to let her go. Dr. McKay put a hand on his arm.

"It's okay son," he said as if he were speaking to a member of his own family. "She'll be okay." Tom nodded, his heart breaking for the woman he loved. The two men stood quietly in the corner of the room where Lisa now sat with the dying dog. She had drawn a chair up next to the examining table and was cradling the soft black head in her hands. She whispered softly, all the while stroking the matted fur.

"You are a good dog, Sadie. A good dog. You did a wonderful job bringing those puppies into the world. They're fine pups, and they're all going to grow up into wonderful dogs who will love their people just the way you have loved Millie. Millie wanted to be here, Sadie, but she's sick too. I know she is thinking about you and sending her love. She loves you girl with all of her heart. You'll never be forgotten. You are a good dog Sadie. A good dog. You can rest now. You can let go. It's okay. It's your time. Good bye Sadie." A strangled sob escaped Lisa's lips as she felt the beautiful dog relax. Sadie had taken her last breath. Lisa dropped her head and rested it there for a few minutes and then rose to finish her tears into Tom's shoulder.

Chapter Twelve

After a couple of minutes, Tom gently led Lisa out into the clinic lobby. She sank slowly down on one of the padded benches while Tom went to speak to the vet who was entering information into a computer behind the counter. Tom spoke quietly, hoping Lisa wouldn't hear. "What happens now?" Tom asked.

The old vet rubbed his stubbly chin and pushed his glasses back up onto his nose. "We'll have to make arrangements for the body. Normally I can ask the owner how they want to do things, but in this case....I'm not sure what to do."

"What do most people do?" Tom asked. This was all new to him.

"These days most folks ask for private cremation and have the ashes returned to them for burial at a place of their choosing. Do you think Lisa would consider speaking to Millie and asking what she wants to do?" Tom shrugged, totally at a loss for words. All of this was so emotionally draining for Lisa. He wondered if she could handle delivering this news to Millie as well.

"Guess all I can do is ask?" He headed back to where Lisa sat, wiping her eyes. She looked so sad, all Tom wanted to do was take her in his arms and make all the hurt go away. He had never had pets growing up, so he was finding all this emotion somewhat overwhelming. In the years that he and Lisa had been together he had grown to love Bear, and he was beginning to appreciate the human and animal connection. He never realized that it was something that went far beyond a love for one's own pets. Apparently, well in Lisa's case anyway, a compassion for animals seemed to extend to all pets, hers and anyone else's. She looked up with red rimmed eyes and took his extended hand. Tom sat close beside her and kept her hands in his.

 "Dr. McKay needs to know what to do with the body. He was wondering if you wanted to ask Millie what her final wishes might be. Private cremation is apparently what most people choose." Lisa thought for a moment, nodding her agreement.

"It's what I have always chosen for my pets, and I'm sure it's what Millie would want too." She started to say more, but then stopped.

"What is it?" Tom prodded.

Lisa looked at him with fresh tears threatening to fall. "Private cremation is not cheap. I don't think Millie has the kind of money it would take. She may have to refuse to do it for economic reasons, and I think that would break her heart."

"But she should be consulted anyway don't you think?" Tom was pretty sure he knew where Lisa was headed with her train of thought.

Lisa looked at him and pleaded. "No, I think we should just make the arrangement with Dr. McKay and cover the cost ourselves. I just don't want her to have to make that decision in her current state. It's bad enough that she has to deal with the loss at all." Tom nodded.

"I'll go tell the Doc. You gather yourself together and then we'll go visit Millie again." Dr. McKay agreed to make the arrangements, and also agreed to let the pup stay on at the clinic one more night.

Millie was dozing as they entered the room but she opened her eyes quickly at the sound of their approaching footsteps. "So how is she? How's my girl?" The hope in the old tired eyes was almost more than Lisa could bear. She took a deep breath and perched on the edge of the chair that Tom had pulled up next to the bed. Lisa gently covered the frail wrinkled hand that rested on the bed.

"I'm so sorry, Millie. Dr. McKay did everything he could but Sadie was just too weak. She died a little while ago at the clinic. Dr. McKay had made her comfortable. She wasn't in pain at the end, and I stayed with her. I told her how much you loved her and what a good dog she was. I was with her Millie, she wasn't alone. I'm so so sorry." Lisa struggled to stay strong, and held the old woman's hand while a trail of tears followed a wrinkled path down her face. Millie closed her eyes and lay back on the pillows. After a time, she spoke.

"Thank you for being with her. I feel better knowing that she wasn't alone. I just can't believe I'll never see her again."

"I know," Lisa consoled. "Millie, there is one other thing I want you to know. Tom and I made arrangements with the vet to have Sadie privately cremated. Her ashes will be returned to you in about a week. I hope you don't mind us making that choice for you. I didn't want you to have the extra worry right now." Millie smiled gratefully.

"Thank you so much," she whispered. "This way I will have a chance to say goodbye. Thank you for giving me that." Then the blue eyes closed once again and Lisa felt the grip on her hand relax. She gently moved her hand away and pulled the hospital blanket up around the old woman's shoulders. She and Tom tiptoed out of the room.

Once in the hall, Lisa let out a long ragged breath. "There, I'm glad that part's over. Let's go home. I could use a nap myself."

Tom agreed, adding "We'd better rest up 'cause I figure that young pup is going to be full of beans once he gets let out of that crate!" Lisa laughed outright. It was a good sound, and one that Tom was so happy to hear.

Chapter Thirteen

It was amazing what a good night's sleep could do! Lisa woke up refreshed and ready to face the challenges of a new day. A quick glance out the bedroom window lightened her heart even more. The sun was shining and she could hear robins chirping their delight at the prospect of tasty worms emerging from the warm soil, happy that the snow was finally gone. Bear was already outside lying on the floor of the verandah, his face turned towards the sun. She wondered if he had any idea what was in store for him this day, and how he would react to a puppy invading his space. Lisa smiled to herself. Bear was such a softie; it likely wouldn't bother him at all. In fact, he may just be a little rejuvenated by the feisty intruder!

The smell of fresh brewed coffee lured her away from the window. Tom was always the first one up and rare was the morning that coffee wasn't ready and waiting for her. She was a very lucky woman and she knew it. Soon they would be a little family and Lisa could hardly wait. But first things first. For the next few days she had to concentrate on finding the best home for a needy puppy.

Tom sat a cup of the fresh brew at her usual spot at the kitchen table. Lisa cupped the warm mug lovingly and took a long slow sip. "Yummmm," she mumbled. "You do make a good cup of coffee, my love."

"My specialty," he replied waving his arm in an exaggerated bow, before joining her at the table. "So today we pick up a puppy," he said with a more serious tone. "Think you're ready for that?"

"Absolutely," Lisa smiled. "Should be fun. Remind me though, to call the hospital before we go. I want to know how Millie is doing."

They finished coffee and breakfast, and took turns showering and getting ready. While Tom was finishing up, Lisa went out and spent some time with Bear. They walked a short ways into the woods on the wet trail. Bear kept his nose pointed towards the sky as if drinking in all the fresh spring scents. Lisa rested her hand gently on his big head as they walked. "You liking this weather Bear?" she asked. "I bet you are," she answered for the old mutt. They didn't go far. Once the trail took a turn into the deeper woods, it was far too mucky to travel. "Let's head back now, buddy," she said as she changed direction, making sure her furry companion followed suit. "Don't want to lose you again," she said more to herself than to the dog.

Tom was ready to go by the time they got back and was putting the final touches on puppy proofing the house. Lisa had already run through the drill with him. Extension cords, socks, gloves and any small articles of clothing as well as anything food related had to be put safely out of reach. Even though the plan was to keep the puppy short term, Lisa knew the importance of keeping him safe. Puppies could eat or chew something dangerous in the blink of an eye.

"All good in here, I think," Tom announced as Lisa wiped some of the mud from Bear's paws. "We are puppy ready!" They decided to leave Bear at home while they went to retrieve the pup rather than asking Bear to share the rather small back seat. Lisa gave him a chew bone and explained what was happening, even though her words fell on deaf ears. She had always talked a lot to Bear, and she had no intentions of stopping now.

They were about to pull away when Lisa suddenly remembered that she had wanted to call the hospital. "You didn't remind me." She playfully admonished. "I'm the one with pregnant woman brain. You're supposed to help me remember." Lisa laughed at Tom's expression. Between an emotional pregnant wife, a senior dog and a young puppy, the poor guy had a lot to deal with. Lisa loved him for his good nature and his ability to take all these challenges in stride. Secretly, she thought the puppy thing might be his biggest challenge yet!

Lisa ran in to the house and made the call. Tom breathed a sigh of relief when she came back out the front door with a big smile on her face.

"Millie is doing fine," she announced as she settled herself back into her seat as gracefully as her belly would allow. "She is being discharged later today. The nurse said she has a friend coming to take her home."

"Good news," Tom added. "I'm glad she has someone to call on when she needs help."

"Me too," Lisa agreed. "Once we get this puppy business settled, I'd like to go visit her again myself."

"Then let's get this show on the road," Tom said as they pulled onto the highway. "I'm sure that feisty little critter has turned old Doctor McKay into a bundle of nerves!"

Chapter Fourteen

Lisa had to admit she had forgotten how much hard work puppies were. This little guy apparently had the tiniest bladder on earth. It seemed like every time she or Tom sat down, he needed to be let outside, and when they weren't doing that, they were chasing him out of corners where they had tucked away extension cords, or shooing him away from the corners of the coffee table that were right at mouth level. Between those things, and nipping at their slippers with every step they took, puppy parenthood was posing quite a challenge.

Fortunately Bear seemed quite relaxed about his new house guest. After snarling a bit and letting the pup know who was boss, they settled into an unexpected peace. The pup seemed to know that Bear wanted no part of any shenanigans and he happily complied. Tom and Lisa would often find them curled up together in doggy dreamland as though they had been together forever. Those peaceful moments almost gave Lisa pause about keeping the pup….almost. Then she would remind herself of her reasons for not having a puppy right now. Her heart and her head were definitely fighting a battle over this one. She truly hadn't expected Bear to accept the situation so well. And the puppy was so darn cute! Then she would remind herself that a young pup and a newborn might be biting off just a little more than she could chew right now. No, they would have to find a good foster home for the little guy. That's all there was to it. She was deep in thought about that when Tom came into the kitchen, notebook in hand.

"I think I've narrowed it down to two possibilities. Mighty Mutts Dog Rescue and Furever Homes Dog Rescue. In both cases the dogs are placed in foster homes for as long as it takes to find the right match. They have pretty strict criteria too, for people adopting dogs. They arrange several home visits to make sure that the dog will be a good fit for the family before the dog is placed permanently. I think either one sounds good. Do you think we should plan a visit for later today?"

Lisa hesitated before answering. "Yes, I guess so." Tom raised an eyebrow.

"Are you having second thoughts about giving him up? Are you thinking maybe you'd like to keep him after all?"

"No. I mean I was….kind of. But, no. It's just not a good time right now. Let's go visit them both today. Do you think they'll be able to take him in right away?"

Tom gave a little shrug. "The web site didn't really say. It's more focused on the dogs they have available for adoption than anything else. I'll call and get things started." Then, turning back to Lisa he added, "If you're sure, that is."

"Yes I'm sure. Like you said, he's going to be an easy dog to place. Just look at him!" They both watched in amusement as a blur of black and white fur raced around the coffee table in pursuit of a big rubber ball. "He'll make a wonderful pet for some family!" Tom nodded and went to the kitchen to make the calls. Lisa sat on the floor and rolled the ball for the pup to chase in hopes of wearing him down before they put him in the car. Bear dozed on his bed in front of the fire, oblivious to all the commotion. Tom returned to the living room announcing that they had appointments for both places that afternoon. Lisa ruffled the pup's fur, and cradling his tiny head in both her hands she talked to him softly.

"Okay, little man. You are going to meet some new people today and I want you to be on your best behavior okay? Can you be a good dog and show everybody how smart and friendly you are?" The pup licked her face in response. Lisa laughed as she pushed him gently away. "That's enough kisses, thank you," she laughed.

The chime of the phone interrupted their playtime and Tom went to answer. Lisa could hear him chatting in a pleasant tone, so she knew it wasn't a telemarketer or a salesperson. Her curiosity got the better of her and she rose from the floor to go investigate, the little pup nipping at her slippers all the way. When she reached the kitchen, Tom was just saying goodbye.

"It was the supervisor from the food bank asking if we had found the woman with the dog. I let her know that everything was fine, and thanked her again for her help."

"It was nice of her to call," Lisa said.

"It was," Tom agreed. "But we had better get going. I'm not sure exactly where this place is, so I want to give ourselves some extra time." The pup wasted no time grabbing for one of his slippers as he changed them out for his boots.

They found the Mighty Mutts Rescue without any trouble at all. It was located just outside of town in what was once a small storefront. The sounds of dogs barking came from a fenced in area at the back of the building. Inside, there was just a small reception area furnished with what looked like someone's second hand furniture, and a door that led to back rooms that held several dog kennels of various sizes. The kennels were all empty, and a young woman in colorful scrubs was mopping the floor. At the sound of the door closing, she turned to greet them. "Make yourselves comfortable," she called as she put her cleaning utensils away. "Be right out."

Tom and Lisa sat on the loveseat closest to the door and kept the pup reigned in close. He was shivering and hiding behind Tom's legs. New places and people were still frightening for him and he saw Tom as his protector. The young woman's face erupted in a huge grin when she saw the pup. "Well aren't you a handsome fellow," she said, bending down and getting nose to nose with him. The pup instantly sensed that she was a friend and began licking her all over. She ruffled his fur for a few more minutes before finally standing and introducing herself to Tom and Lisa.

"Hi, Jennifer Briggs," she said extending her hand. "You must be Tom and Lisa. Welcome to Mighty Mutts." Tom and Lisa shook hands and smiled, both pleased at such a warm and genuine greeting. They chatted for a while and eventually left with a very positive opinion of the organization. Their next stop, at Furever Homes Dog Rescue was an equally pleasant experience. Again the volunteers were friendly, knowledgeable and genuinely interested in finding good homes for their furry clients.

Lisa wondered how they would decide which one to choose. The only factor playing a big part in their decision was that Mighty Mutts had some vacancies available right away, while Furever Homes had asked if they could keep the pup a few more days while they screened a couple of new foster homes. They left Furever Homes planning to discuss things over lunch, promising to get back to both places with a decision as soon as possible. In the end, they saw no reason to wait. Mighty Mutts was a terrific organization, and Lisa really wanted to get things settled. They left the restaurant and headed back to see Jennifer Briggs at Mighty Mutts to make the final arrangements.

Chapter Fifteen

Lisa hung her coat in the closet and put her boots on the shelf underneath. As she slid her feet into her slippers without the hassle of fighting off little puppy teeth, she marveled at how quickly the little pup had wormed his way into her heart and her life. A bit of sadness tugged at her heart, both for the puppy they left today, and for the old dog who would be leaving them someday soon. At that moment, she felt the baby do a gentle roll as if to remind her of happier times to come. Rubbing her belly, she smiled and headed in to give Bear a big hug. "Hey big fella," she cooed, hugging his scruffy neck. "Life is back to normal. For now anyway. But you'd better enjoy the peace while you have it. Things are going to get a lot busier around here!" As if he understood, Bear lowered his mighty head back onto his paws and closed his eyes. He could sense Lisa's happiness though, and her love. That was everything he needed to be happy.

The next few days were spent getting back to the normal routine of life. Tom returned to work, and Lisa continued with baby plans. She washed and folded tiny little shirts and sleepers. She organized and shopped, went to her OB appointments and read every baby magazine she could get her hands on. She and Bear went for lazy walks on the trail that was drying gradually with the warm spring temperatures. The snow was completely gone now, and an array of colorful song birds had joined the robins digging for worms and seeds. Bear walked a little slower every day it seemed, but never hesitated when the opportunity came for an outing. He was indeed enjoying the spring just as Lisa had hoped he would.

They were just coming in from a recent walk when the phone rang in the kitchen. Lisa slipped out of her rain boots and went to answer, glancing behind her to make sure that Bear had followed her in and that the door had closed behind her.

"Hello," she said cheerily into the handset. She was greeted by Dr. McKay's deep voice.

"Lisa, It's Dr. McKay. I just wanted to let you know that Sadie's ashes have been returned to us. I was wondering if you or Tom would be picking them up or if I should be contacting her owner."

Lisa responded quickly. "I don't think Millie would be able to get into town. I'll come by this afternoon and get them."

"Fine, fine. I'll see you later then."

"Yes you will and thank you for calling." Lisa plunked the handset back into its base and started thinking about Millie. As hard as this was going to be, Lisa was pretty sure she'd be happy to have Sadie home again. She wondered where Sadie's final resting place would be. It wasn't long before her train of thought skipped from Millie and Sadie to herself and Bear. Where would she choose to have Bear rest? It would have to be somewhere nearby. She wanted to always feel as though Bear were with her. Deciding that thinking about it just made her too sad, Lisa forced herself to think of something else. If she was going to go out to Millie's she should call first and make sure it was okay. Lisa debated whether to tell Millie that she was bringing Sadie with her or not. "If it was me," Lisa thought to herself. "I'd want to know." She picked up the handset once again and searched through her desk for Millie's number. The phone rang a number of times and Lisa was about to hang up when Millie finally answered. Lisa explained why she was calling and waited patiently when there was a long silence on the other end. Maybe Millie wasn't ready for the shock of having her beloved pet returned to her. Then a quiet voice said simply, "Yes, today would be fine. I'll see you this afternoon." The click of the receiver told Lisa the conversation was over, but not before Lisa detected the unmistakable sound of tears in the old woman's voice. This wasn't going to be easy, for either of them. Before she left, Lisa called Tom and told him where she was going and then hurried to get Bear situated and comfortable. She didn't think he was up to a visit with strangers, plus getting him in and out of the car was getting more and more difficult. Better that he stay home safe and sound. Lisa fluffed up his blanket and settled him with a chew bone. Patting his head, she told him she would be back soon.

A young girl she hadn't met before was manning the counter in Dr. McKay's office. Her name tag read Carol and Lisa assumed she was the one the Doctor had said was away after some damage on her property. She looked up and smiled as Lisa approached. Lisa returned her smile and introduced herself.

The girl nodded as she listened. "Dr. McKay filled me in on the whole thing. I'm so glad your dog was found and all those puppies were rescued."

"Thanks, "Lisa replied. "Except for poor Sadie, it all worked out pretty well." Carol's smile faded.

"Yes, poor girl. But at least we found out where she belongs. And that's why you are here, right?" Lisa nodded. "One second, I'll be right back." Carol disappeared into the back room only to emerge in just a few seconds with a pastel blue box. "Here is Sadie," she sighed. "Please tell her owner how sorry we are for her loss."

"I will," Lisa promised, taking the box with a heavy heart. This box contained so much more than just ashes. This box contained the memories of an entire lifetime of love, loyalty and companionship. It was the heaviest box Lisa had ever carried. She hurried to say her goodbyes before her tears got the better of her. Once settled in the car, she let them come. She cried for Sadie. She cried for Millie and she cried for herself, dreading the day that she would bring home yet another box that would weigh even heavier on her heart than this one.

After a few minutes, Lisa dried her eyes and gathered herself together for the trip to Millie's. She was going to have to be strong to help Millie through this. It was a good thing she had already had her meltdown. Pulling into Millie's driveway, Lisa was happy to see the old woman on the porch enjoying the warm sunshine. The windows of the cabin were open, letting the fresh air inside and Lisa could tell how much more cheerful the place looked than it had on her last visit. Millie looked a lot better too. There was some color in her cheeks and as she rose to greet her, Lisa thought how much stronger she looked. Lisa opened the back door of the car to retrieve the blue box from the back seat. Millie's eyes filled as she watched, and she ran a hand gently over the box, before taking it from Lisa trembling hands. Millie carried the box back to her chair and settled it in her lap. Her eyes took on a faraway expression and Lisa waited quietly for her to speak. Finally she turned to Lisa and thanked her for returning Sadie to her.

"I think I'll bury her ashes right here in my garden," she said at last. "And I'll plant some special flowers just for her. When I watch those flowers grow and bloom I'll remember my Sadie and all the wonderful years we had together." Lisa couldn't speak. Suddenly Millie snapped out of her reveries and spoke in a strong voice.

"Now, where are my manners? Please, come sit and I'll get us a drink. Lemonade maybe?"

"That would be lovely," Lisa said, trying to make her voice more cheerful than she felt while she settled into the chair beside Millie's. Millie took the blue box with her when she went in to get the drinks and that was the last Lisa saw of it. From here on, it was Millie's task to undertake.

The two women chatted for a while about this and that, and then Millie asked about Sadie's pups.

"So they all went to good homes? All three of them?"

"Well, two of them so far," Lisa explained. "We took the third one to Mighty Mutts Dog Rescue. They were going to place him in a foster home until they could find the perfect forever home for him."

Millie's eyes grew large and she looked somewhat shocked. "You gave him up?" she asked.

"We just couldn't take a puppy in right now. We were very careful where he went. We made sure he was in caring hands. I'm sorry if this upsets you, Millie" Lisa said with genuine regret. "We were assured that he would go to a loving home."

For a long time Millie sat in silence. Her words were filled with sadness when she finally spoke. "I would have taken him," she said. "It would have meant a lot to me to have one of Sadie's pups." Lisa's hand flew to her mouth as fresh tears threatened to fall.

"Oh, Millie. I'm so sorry. It never even occurred to me. I'm so sorry. Of course you would want to have one of her pups. I don't know why I didn't think of that. "

Millie tried to console her, but she was almost just as upset as Lisa. "It's alright, dear," she comforted. "How could you have known? I was so sick when you saw me last. Not the best candidate for puppy motherhood! And truth be told, if it was any other than one of Sadie's pups, I might not have even considered it."

Lisa's mind was whirling. Maybe it wasn't too late. Maybe she could get the pup back for Millie. She had to try. She shared her thoughts with Millie, while she gathered her things together to leave. "I'm going to head over there right now and see what I can do," she called, already starting he engine.

Chapter Sixteen

"I'm sorry, Lisa, said Jennifer when Lisa arrived at Mighty Mutts. "The pup was placed in a foster home right after you dropped him off. We like to get the dogs into foster care as soon as possible. We don't really have the space or the staff to keep them here for very long."

"Can I go retrieve him from the foster home then? The woman who owned his mother really wants to have him." Lisa didn't like the look of hesitation on the woman's face. Jennifer Briggs was a very friendly person, but Lisa quickly got a sense that you really didn't want to put a dog's best interest into question. She was obviously very passionate about her work.

"But didn't you tell me originally that the woman was in ill health and hadn't been able to care for the mother dog and the pups in the first place? Why should we think that she is the best person to have this pup now?"

"Yes, that is all true, but she's out of hospital now, and doing well. She lives alone and the pup would be great company for her. She lost the mother dog and is feeling pretty lonely." Jennifer still didn't look convinced.

"I just don't know if it's a good idea. That pup has already been through a lot. If we place him with her and it doesn't work out, he'll have to adjust all over again."

"You are absolutely right, and I agree with all of that. But I also believe in my heart that this is the right thing to do. I intend to stay in touch with Millie so I'll be able to help her out with some of the things she couldn't manage on her own. I'll take full responsibility for monitoring the situation. The pup will know me and if it doesn't work out, Tom and I will take the pup in. He won't have to undergo any further stress. Please say you agree!"

Jennifer smiled and threw her hands up in a gesture of submission. "Ok, you win. Just let me give the foster Mom a call and let her know you're coming." Lisa clapped her hands together like a little kid receiving her most asked for birthday gift.

"You won't regret this. I promise."

In a few minutes Lisa was on her way across town to the foster home. She was excited to get the pup and head out to Millie's place. She couldn't wait to see her face when she arrived with the pup. Lisa made a mental note to stop at the pet store on her way and get some supplies for Millie. She would buy her a new dog bed, a good start up stock of quality kibble, and a few snacks and toys. This pup might very well surpass even Bear for being the most spoiled dog on earth! Lisa laughed as she drove along imagining just what a wonderful life this dog was going to have. Then, thinking that Tom might want to know what was going on, she pushed the call button on her Bluetooth and reached him at his office. Lisa was a little bummed at the hesitation in his voice.

"What's wrong? Do you think this is a bad idea?"

Tom chose his words carefully, sensing the defensive tone in Lisa's voice. "I'm just worried about you, honey. Are you sure you want to take this on right now? You've been through a lot lately and with the baby and all......" he let his sentence trail off. Lisa really didn't want this to become an argument, and she didn't want it to shadow their happy time in any way. She understood, and appreciated Tom's concern.

"I'm absolutely okay with this," she said brightly, making sure there was no hint of doubt in her voice. "I really want to stay in touch with Millie and the pup will be a good incentive. Please, don't worry. I know it's all going to work out for the best." Tom finally agreed, and Lisa said goodbye promising to be home in time to cook him his favorite dinner.

With all of the stops, it seemed like it was taking forever to get to Millie's house. The pup was new to being in a car and was having trouble settling in his crate. His whimpering and pleading puppy dog eyes made the trip seem even longer. Lisa talked to him while she drove, just as she always did to Bear. She honestly wondered sometimes if all dog owners talked to their pets as much as she did.

Millie's door opened the second she heard the sound of tires on the gravel. Lisa was relieved to see how healthy she looked. And the smile of anticipation on her face was worth every second that Lisa had spent on this whole entire project. Millie continued on down the steps and waited while Lisa pulled to a stop. Then she was at the back window of the car, peering into the eyes of the dog who would be her companion for the next however many years. Both women had tears in their eyes as Lisa opened the back door.

"Oh, just look at you!" Millie crooned. "You look just like your Mama." The pup was on his feet and wriggling around in his confined space. "Well let's get you out of there."

"Here, let me," Lisa offered, as she slid the crate forward and then lifted it out of the car. She sat the crate on the ground and bent as best she could over her pregnant belly to open the door. The pup nearly knocked her onto her backside in his eagerness to be free. He jumped up and put both paws on her lap, licking her face and neck and trying to bite her earrings. Lisa and Millie laughed at his antics. He continued to bound from one to the other of them before deciding to venture off and explore some of his new surroundings.

"I've brought you a few welcome puppy gifts as well," Lisa said as she started unloading the car. At the sight of all the thoughtful items, Millie engulfed Lisa in a big bear hug.

"Thank you so much," she said with tears in her voice. "You have no idea how much this means to me."

"Oh yes, I do," Lisa said, smiling. They passed the rest of the afternoon enjoying a cup of cocoa and watching the pup investigate his new home. Lisa parted with the agreement to return in a few days for another visit. She didn't mention anything about the conversation she had had with Jennifer Briggs, or Tom, or her intentions to be this new puppy's secret guardian.

Chapter Seventeen

As promised, Lisa had Tom's favorite dinner of beef stroganoff simmering on the stove when he got home. Over a quiet dinner, with no puppy interruptions, she told him the whole story of the pup's and Millie's introduction to each other.

"You should have seen her face, Tom. She was so happy! I just know that pup is going to make a big difference to her life."

Tom tried to keep the concern out of his voice. "I'm glad. I really am, and I think as long as we keep close tabs on things, everything will work out fine. I'll be over there myself off and on for the next few weeks so I can help out with that." Lisa sent him a look across the table that plainly showed her appreciation and gratitude. As her foot moved under the table and brushed Bear's side, she hoped that the new pup would live the long and happy life that Bear had known.

"So what did Millie name the pup?" Tom asked. Lisa realized that they hadn't even discussed it.

"I haven't the foggiest idea. All she said was that the pup looked just like his Mama. She never said what she wanted to name him. Guess I'll find out on my next visit."

"And when will that be?" Tom continued. "I'll be over there at the end of the week. Think you can wait that long? Then we could go together."

Lisa nodded and agreed. "I have appointments and other chores to do anyway. That should work out fine. "

It was good to get back to the everyday tasks of running a household. Although the last few weeks had been stressful, they had certainly flown by quickly. Lisa could hardly believe that her due date was now less than eight weeks away. By the time summer was over, it would almost be time. She was relaxing by the big picture window when she realized Bear had come and laid down at her feet. She absently stroked his big head with her foot, wondering what he was going to think of the new baby. She had been so focused on not losing him through the winter, that she hadn't thought much about him adjusting to the changes that were coming. She reached down to scratch his ears. "You'll be just fine, won't you big guy? You are such a gentle giant; I have no concerns at all."

Friday morning dawned bright and clear and Lisa woke to the sounds of robins in the maple tree outside her window. It was going to be a good day to visit Millie. They could sit outside in the sunshine and let the pup romp. Bear followed her around as she prepared to leave, always at the ready for a road trip. He didn't get to go very often but in a last minute decision, Lisa decided to bring him along. He would enjoy the outing, and maybe even enjoy seeing his little friend again. By the time the sun was peeking over the pines they were on the road.

Once again Millie stepped onto the porch at the sounds of tires on gravel. Lisa laughed. "Millie doesn't need a doorbell. She always hears everybody coming!" The pup strained at the end of the leash Millie held in her hand. She called to them as they got out of the car. "He doesn't know to stay yet, so I keep him on a leash around moving cars. Do you mind if I let him go now?"

"Sure, let him go." Tom called as he turned to open the back door of the car. "We have a little surprise for him."

The pup made a beeline for the new arrivals but put the brakes on full stop when he watched Bear clamber out of the back seat. He stood perfectly still while Bear sauntered over to him. Then he laid right down on his belly, paws waving in the air, trying to lick Bears jowls at the same time. Bear sniffed him all over and then moved on to relieve himself by the old oak that dominated Millie's front yard. The adults watched with interest as the two dogs did their doggy thing, pleased that there was not going to be any confrontations.

"Good boy, Bear." Lisa said, as the old dog strolled patiently around the yard, the spirited pup hot on his heels.

"So what's the little guy's name?" Tom asked. Millie smiled.

"It took me a long time to come up with a name that suited him," she said shaking her head. "I wanted to get a sense of his personality before I named him but I finally hit on the perfect one. "Hoover, "she stated, rather proudly. "I named him after my old vacuum after I saw him pick up every single crumb, scrap of paper or bit of fluff that hit the floor. He's a Hoover for sure!"

Lisa and Tom both nodded approvingly. "He looks like a Hoover," Lisa agreed.

The day passed in relaxed and pleasant conversation. Tom finished his work repairing the roof, with promises to come back and repair the porch steps on his next visit. "Better to get the roof done first," he said, "Before the summer rains come." Millie thanked him over and over. She thanked Lisa too, for her help with Hoover and for being such a good friend.

"It's our pleasure," Lisa assured her. "We're just glad that everything has turned out so well."

Driving away, Tom reached across the front seat and took Lisa's hand. "I'm so proud of you," he said. "What you did for that little old lady is just remarkable. That pup has literally brought her back to life!"

Lisa laid her head back against the seat and let out a big sigh. "Ya," she said, already starting to drift off. "Dogs have a way of doing that, don't they Bear?"

Epilogue

The last of the fall colors have finally faded and the world is taking on that muted shade of gray that precedes winter. Lisa stands at the big picture window as she often does, watching the weather, her thoughts projecting ahead to another long winter. It will be a different winter than she has ever experienced before. She looks down at the tiny bundle in her arms.

"This will be your first winter, little one," she says. "Your first snow, your first Christmas, your first sleigh ride. I can't wait to share it all with you." Her eyes travel across the yard to the big perennial garden where all the color has faded except for one small bush that remains a bright shade of yellowy green even this late in the season. A small bronze statue of a fluffy dog sits at the base of that bush looking out across the yard. The engraved plate on the statue says simply, "Bear. Always loved. Always remembered." Lisa eyes fill with tears when they fall upon the sculpture and she hugs the tiny bundle a little closer.

A little ways out of town, at the end of a long gravel driveway, another woman looks out her door and across the wide expanse of her property. Her face shows the wear and tear of many a long winter, but her eyes are still bright with anticipation, as though wondering what each new day might bring. She too, holds a bundle in her arms, albeit a furry one. She puts her cheek to the soft muzzle and is rewarded with a sloppy kiss. She also has a similar statue in her yard, protected by the sweeping branches of a majestic oak. The plaque around this small dog's neck reads simply,

"Sadie. Forever in my Heart."   She puts her furry friend down and opens the front door. She smiles as she watches the blur of black and white fur race by in pursuit of a chipmunk long gone into hiding. "I wonder what you're going to think of snow," she laughs. At the sound of her laughter, the small head turns in her direction, gives up the futile chase and runs full speed ahead, dropping at her feet for a belly rub.

The End

Thank you so much for purchasing this book. It is readers like you who make the writing process all worthwhile. I hope if you enjoyed these stories that you will consider leaving a review at Amazon.

I always enjoy hearing from my readers. You can contact me at danalandersbooks@gmail.com. I read and respond to all my emails.

In Loving Memory of Riley

2000-2013

Printed in Great Britain
by Amazon